EXCEPTIONAL
An Amazing Story of a Dog Named Salli

A work of fiction by Larry Morris

A story of a very special dog's love, devotion, bravery and protection.

> "If there are no dogs in heaven,
> then when I die,
> I want to go where they went."
>
> Will Rogers

This book is dedicated to:

The volunteers that give countless hours of their time to care for dogs that need our help. Today, thousands of dogs are finding forever homes because of your dedication.

Thank You!

＼ ＼ ＼ ＼ ＼ ＼ ＼ ＼ ＼

Copyright 2020, by

Larry Morris

All rights reserved

CHAPTER 1

After helping with dinner clean-up, Doug started his after-dinner walk. He had done this daily for years. It helped with digesting the meal and keeping him in better health. Now, Doug Thomas owned a landscape business, which had become fairly successful over the years, so it wasn't like he didn't get enough exercise through his work to stay in shape, but he found an evening walk to be cathartic, so he'd kept up the routine. Still, he made a point of returning within thirty minutes so he could round out the night with his family. He felt he was a very lucky guy: still in love with the woman, Alicia, he married 19 years ago, raising two great kids with her, Robbie 12 and Chloe 8, and everyone enjoying good health.

He walked a specific route most every evening; he varied it up some so as not to get bored, but always started by walking up the long hill just a couple blocks from his house. That got his heart rate up and he could feel it in his legs so he knew it was doing some good. He made a point to walk on the left side of the road so he could see the traffic coming toward him. During the fall and winter, he always carried a flashlight so he could see and be seen. He didn't worry too much when he was on the sidewalk, but part of the hill didn't have sidewalk, leaving him to navigate the roadside shoulder.

On this particular night, as Doug stepped off the sidewalk and turned to continue up the shoulder, which sloped off gradually on the verge into a deep ditch, the flashlight passed over something that caught his eye. He thought it looked like a tail, so he stepped closer to the ditch, pushed back some of the tall grass, and discovered in the beam of his light the body of a full-grown dog lying dead on the ground down below.

The temperature in Oregon that night was hovering around 38 degrees, cold enough for Doug to think he should report finding the dog to the police, rather than going all the way down and checking its collar for ID. He shone the light on the dog again to see what breed it was, or at least what color and markings it had. He was somewhat familiar with dogs, and it looked to him like a pit bull. As he scanned the light over its lifeless body he suddenly noticed a puppy lying close to the dead dog's head. His heartbeat rose.

Directing the flashlight's beam around the scene

with the precision of a scalpel, Doug soon spied another puppy lying a bit further away. He decided he would make his way down to where they lay just to be sure there wasn't another puppy his survey had missed. He carefully inched down to the bottom of the ditch, stepping over the water that lay at its base, then climbed up on the other side to where the dogs were.

He put his hand on the adult dog and found it ice cold. The body was becoming stiff but Doug was able to determine the sex as female, but unable to find any visible signs of identification on her. The two puppies his light had revealed were also cold and stiff. He scoured the area with the flashlight and saw another puppy lying a few feet away, also appearing dead. As he reached down to move it closer to its mother, he suddenly jerked back. There, just inches away, sat another puppy staring at Doug. It held no expression, made no sound, just issued a blank stare directly into Doug's face. Doug felt his heart racing and somehow afraid to reach out toward the dog.

He took a few deep breaths and said out loud to the puppy, "You scared the shit out of me little fella."

As soon as Doug recovered from the scare, it became clear to him that something had to be done quickly to help this last dog survive. First he swept the light over the rest of the surrounding ground to be certain it held no more puppies. Stretching out his left arm, he tenderly took the stoic pup by the knap of the neck and lifted it to his lap. He checked to see if there were any external injuries; none were visible. He identified that the dog was female. He knew he had to get her warm quickly for any hope of survival.

Doug had on a t-shirt, a golf shirt, a sweat shirt, and a heavy coat, along with gloves and a stocking cap. He started to put the dog inside his coat but quickly realized that wasn't going to be enough so he unzipped his coat, lifted up his t-shirt, shirt and sweatshirt and put the puppy spread eagle on his bare chest. He then tucked in all the shirts and zipped up his coat so the puppy's bare chest was directly contacted his own. He glanced down into the cave of protection; the puppy's expression had not changed, yet she continued to stare directly into Doug's eyes.

"Let's see if we can get you through this, baby girl."

He climbed carefully out of the ditch and headed back home, pulling the sweatshirt up to cover the puppy's head but give her enough room to breathe, then once on the road walked briskly to keep his and her body temperature up.

When he entered the house he heard Alisha say

from the kitchen, "How was the walk hon? You got back a little quicker than usual, did ya freeze out?"

"Lish, come here babe, I need your help."

She came around the corner and saw the little head of the dog sticking out from his shirt, uttering, "What the hell…"

"I found her and her dead mother lying in a ditch. There were three other puppies that didn't make it, but this one seems to be pretty damned resilient. Still, she's ice cold."

Alisha moved to action, cranking up the heat in the house and retrieving a small dish towel to put over the heat vent in the kitchen. "Here, put her down on this towel so the heat from the vent is on her. Good, now put your sweatshirt over the top of her."

Alisha grabbed milk from the refrigerator and started heating it up on the stove top. As soon as it got warm she put it into a small glass and got an eyedropper from the medicine cabinet. Doug started tenderly feeding the dog.

This whole time the pup just kept staring at Doug. Finally after taking a few droppers of milk she lay down on the towel, closed her eyes and fell asleep. By this time the kids had learned of the situation and of course came to help. They sweet-talked and petted her to the point that

Doug finally told them to let her be; assuring them they could check her come morning.

After they went to their rooms Doug sat with the vulnerable pup; she seemed content to sleep as the warmth of the vent soothed her frigid frame. Alisha came and sat down next to him. "What do ya think?" she wondered aloud. "She got a chance?"

"I don't know. If she makes it through the night we can take her to the vet first thing in the morning. She seems to be a tough one. In fact she scared the hell out of me, all of her family was dead but she just was sitting there staring at me. I hope she makes it, she seems determined. I like her."

Alisha kissed him on the forehead and said, "Let's keep our fingers crossed till morning."

"Yea, it's about all we can do. I'm going to sleep here tonight to be close. Tell the kids goodnight for me."

Alisha just smiled at him.

CHAPTER 2

Doug kept up his vigil till midnight, but eventually got a little sleep on the couch in earshot of where the dog lay. He awoke at his normal hour of 6 AM, and started to get up to go check on the puppy. He was startled again to find her sitting on the carpet not 2 feet from the couch, just staring at him.

"Hey baby girl! Feeling better this morning? You must be, in order to scare the shit out of me again." He reached down, picked her up and set her in his lap. She felt warm and for that he was thankful. He sat for a moment petting her as she continued to stare into his eyes. He then went to the kitchen and warmed some milk and dropper-fed her again. This time she showed a little enthusiasm, actually suckling on the dropper.

Doug made sure he didn't over feed her and then said, "Let's see if we can get you into see the vet today." He held her until 8 AM, when the vet office opened. After he explained the circumstances the vet agreed to fit them in first thing.

After giving Alisha and the kids a quick update, he made it to the vet's by 8:30, where they got him and his canine ward immediately into an exam room. The vet immediately confirmed that the dog appeared to be an American Pit Bull Terrier, approximately four weeks old. She examined the puppy thoroughly and said, "Frankly, she seems fine. Everything appears normal. I am going to give her a shot with a low dose of antibiotics just in case of an infection, but I don't see any real issues. I'll get you some puppy formula to feed her instead of milk, a can of solid food to give her in small doses, and some liquid vitamins. Bring her back if anything goes wrong in the near term, and I think it would be wise to bring her in again in two weeks for a recheck."

The vet smiled at Doug, "Considering what she went through, she's clearly a tough little cookie."

Doug thanked her and paid for the visit and supplies. As he got into the car he put the blanket he'd brought along into the passenger seat and carefully laid the puppy down on it. She responded with a lick on the hand and a tail wag. Doug was pleased with that and the outcome of the exam.

Back home he explained everything to his wife and kids. They all enthusiastically pitched in to prepare formula and help nurse the puppy back to full health. Doug called the police to report where the dead mother and other puppies were. The police said they would contact animal control and see if they could find out anything, but nothing ever came of it. Doug and his family had a new dog.

*****

After a few weeks of loving attention, the puppy started to interact more. She would play with the kids and her tail wagged a lot. She started to become part of the family, including sleeping with Doug and Alisha on their bed at night. The kids wanted her to sleep with them but she always preferred being closest to Doug.

Soon enough came the inevitable question of a name. The family convened to throw out ideas. After a few minutes, Chloe sheepishly said, "You know, Dad, she kinda looks like Aunt Sally."

Everyone looked at each other for a few seconds, and then started laughing before Doug said, "You know she's right, she does look like aunt Sal."

A still-giggling Alisha said, "We're not naming the dog after your aunt Sally."

"Why not? Take a closer look, she's right, this pup is Sally's doggy doppelganger."

Chloe laughed and looked the puppy right in the face and said, "Yes, you look like a Sally don't you, yes you do, and you'd be a good Sally, wouldn't you?"

The Pup barked and wagged her tail as she turned in circles in an excited motion.

Alisha relented. "OK, OK, but let's spell it with an *i* at the end instead of a *y*."

Doug smiled at her and said, "An *i*? How come?"

"I just remembered a story my Mom used to read to me when I was small. There was a princess in that story that spelled her name with an *i*, Dalli. It was one of my favorite stories."

Everyone agreed and said, "Then an *i* it shall be."

And so began the story of Salli.

CHAPTER 3

Doug researched American Pit Bulls and realized quickly that, in addition to regular exercise, consistent training was going to be a necessity with Salli. Over the years Pit Bulls had gained a reputation of being mean and aggressive. His research found that some Pit Bulls were bred to be fighters and others to be family companion dogs. In today's world most had a little of both sides in them. Pit Bulls are large strong dogs that are generally friendly and affectionate. However, they do have natural tendencies toward aggression, especially when it comes to protection of themselves and their families. That aggressive instinct has to be managed, and the owner of the dog is the one who has to instill that.

Doug got proper instruction from a friend who trained dogs in the military. So early on the puppy started a rigorous training schedule, taught to obey the rules from day one. Salli quickly adapted to the commands and instinctively knew her role in the family. What surprised Doug was the ease with which she responded to every command; it was as though she knew what was expected and never forgot the rules regardless of her excitement or the forgetfulness of the trainer.

*****

After about 6 months, Salli was a regular part of the family. Her routine was adapted to everyone's schedules: When Doug was at work and the kids at school, she stayed close to Alisha. When Alisha worked and she was home alone, she simply waited until someone returned. She was always glad to see the kids come home and loved playing with them. She got excited every time the hour of Doug's nightly (and occasional morning) walks came around.

Doug always used this time to solidify Salli's training and get her some vigorous exercise. He marveled at how well behaved she always was. Generally a 7-month-old puppy could be relied upon to forget their training in excitement or actively test the trainer's boundaries, but Salli seemed to perfectly comprehend how she was expected to act and never failed to act that way.

Even with other dogs she showed no jealousy, aggression or impatience. She would, with permission, play with other animals but whenever they became overly playful or dominant, Salli would, non-violently, do what was necessary to avoid conflict. One time a rather mean-tempered Chihuahua, widely considered the scourge of the neighborhood, attacked Salli and bit her ear. The bite drew blood and Salli yipped in pain. Doug quickly moved in to prevent the scene he expected to follow, but Salli just sat down in front of the Chihuahua and stared into his face. The much littler dog continued to bark and charge, but Salli just stared with a deeply intense look Doug had seen many times. The Chihuahua suddenly stopped barking, sat down in front of Salli and looked down at the ground. Salli then gave a single, subdued *woof* and the Chihuahua looked up at Salli, who wagged her tail and continued her walk.

As Salli grew, her chest widening in muscularity, her head punctuated by a wide jaw and those penetrating eyes more people started actively avoiding her when they saw her coming their way. Doug was disappointed, but did understand, having himself been wary of the breed in the past. But in his heart he knew Salli was not a mean dog and that she wouldn't be involved in any aggressive incidents. After all the time he'd spent with her, he could see the dog thrived on human approval. However, he was careful to respect others' perspectives and always kept an eye on his most unusual dog.

CHAPTER 4

Doug extended his respectful caution around Salli to his and Alisha's family who lived nearby. Alisha's brother Allen and his wife Jennifer had two little ones ages 2 and 4, while her divorced sister Mary traveled extensively as a flight attendant. Doug's sister Julianne , also traveled extensively from her Portland home with her wealthy businessman husband Clark, though they rarely missed spending holidays with Doug and family. His sister Melissa, on the other hand, lived right in town and was a more steady connection. After her divorce, raising a 7-year-old son on a retail sales wage, she relied a lot on Doug and spent a lot of time with him and his family.

They all supported Doug's decision about Salli, but not without a few raised eyebrows. Once there was an incident when Alicia's brother and family were over. With such young children, Allen and Jennifer were naturally a bit concerned about Salli. They had played and spent time with her when she was a puppy, but as she grew in size and strength they became more skeptical about their kids being around what was now a nearly 60 pound Pit Bull.

And so it happened that, after a wonderful dinner, the adults retired to the living room for wine and more conversation. Everyone was having a good time when it suddenly dawned on them that they hadn't seen the children in a while. Panic came over Jennifer's face as she quickly rose to check on them. Doug accompanied her to the kitchen, drawn by the sound of Salli eating. The sight they beheld left them both stunned.

Salli was lying on her stomach in front of her food dish, which was in the hands of Candice, Jennifer's 4-year-old. Kathleen, the 2-year-old, was sitting on Salli's neck, maintaining her balance by holding onto the dog's ears. Candice was taking the food out of the dish a piece at a time and aligning it on the floor in a pattern clearly meaningful to her and her alone. While all this was going on, Salli lay perfectly still, except for the constant wagging of her tail.

Jennifer quickly reached down and picked up Kathleen, and nestled her into her chest as she knelt next to Candice and removed the dish from her hand. As she started to talk to her children, Salli stood up and kissed both children on the face with a warm and sloppy lick. The 2-year-old responded by patting Salli vigorously on the head, while the 4-year-old leaned out and kissed her on the nose.

Jennifer gawped at Doug. "Wow. She actually seems more interested in the kids than her food. She was absolutely calm and understanding of both of them."

Doug nodded, "She is a very sweet dog, but even I'm a bit taken back by this. Usually a dog does not like to be bothered when eating, but she seems actually happy about it."

Jennifer took the kids back into the front room. Doug scooped up Salli's food and returned it to her dish. He told her with a pat on the head that she was a good girl and to go ahead and eat. It suddenly struck Doug to try an experiment. As Sallie started eating, her nose was buried in the dish, Doug stuck his hand directly into the dish and gently pushed her away from her meal. Salli backed away, sat down and waited.

Whoa.

Doug stood, gave the command for "eat" again, washed his hands and went into the front room with the others. When Salli was done eating, she too came into the room, where everyone was sitting and talking. This would be normal, but she was carrying her dish in her mouth. She dropped it in front of the children and spent the rest of the evening playing with them.

Doug was fascinated. He watched closely as the

children playfully grabbed her tail, pulled her ears and even sat atop of her, placing her dish on her head like a crown. Salli showed zero aggravation, impatience or annoyance; in fact, her reaction was quite the opposite. At one point in the evening, the 2-year-old climbed on a table near the couch, which was intended to hold nothing more than a lamp. Before anyone else saw the child getting herself into this fix, Salli was up and at her side, protecting her from an inevitable fall.

Jennifer had spotted her daughter in harm's way seconds before the inevitable, but could only watch. As the table tipped, Salli calmly positioned her head under Kathleen's arm and pressed against her chest as the table toppled. This stopped the table from falling and protected the toddler from hitting the ground. Salli then stood perfectly still as Kathleen began to cry and Jennifer came to the rescue.

Once Jennifer had Kathleen safely on the couch in the comforting arms of her daddy, she knelt down in front of Salli and kissed the dog. Salli reciprocated with a woof and a return kiss. She looked at Doug and said, "I think this one is exceptional!"

CHAPTER 5

Another strange event happened to the Thomas family one evening when they were watching TV. The kids had gone to bed and Salli was on the couch relaxing between Doug and Alisha. A sitcom was on and the volume was loud enough so that neither of them had to strain to hear it. The door to the hallway that lead to the bedrooms was closed, to help keep the noise down for the kids.

Suddenly, for no apparent reason, Salli jerked awake from her sleep, stared at the closed hallway door and tilted her head as if listening to a conversation. Doug and Alisha were startled and looked at her, awaiting a reaction. Salli quickly jumped down and headed to the closed door, tilting her head in a completely focused stance. After a few seconds she turned to Doug and began barking in a loud and frantic way that told Doug not to ignore or shush her.

He and Alisha were immediately on their feet, rushing toward the closed door. When they opened it, Salli sprinted down the hallway to

Chloe's bedroom and began scratching and barking at the closed door. Doug quickly opened the door, revealing Chloe in the throes of a seizure. Both parents were dumbfounded; nothing like this had ever happened to their daughter, and neither knew what to do. Alisha grabbed Chloe's shoulders and began screaming, "Chloe, Chloe, wake up baby, tell me what's going on." Doug held his little girl's ankles, staring at her in open-mouthed, incredulous shock.

Suddenly Salli jumped up on the bed, crawled onto Chloe's stomach and laid full-length on the child with her snout curled under her chin. Alisha instinctively started to pull her off but Salli responded with a very loud and determined bark that made it clear she intended to stay exactly where she was. Alisha implored Doug, "Get her off!"

"No. Leave her," he said. Having regained some of his faculties, he could see that Salli was somehow protecting Chloe from harm by laying on her, providing a calming and supportive presence during the seizure. He also saw that Salli was straddling Chloe so she didn't put too much weight on her body.

"Doug!!"

"No, Alisha, leave her alone. I think she knows what she's doing!"

They both watched as the seizure subsided. Afterward, Salli rose up, licked Chloe on the face, looked directly at Alisha and jumped off the bed. Alisha wrapped her arms around her frightened daughter. "Sweetheart, are you alright?"

"What happened Mom?"

"I don't know, but we are going to take you to the hospital to find out. We will make sure we get you well."

Doug hurried to Robbie's room, woke him and gently told him to get ready to leave. The sleepy boy obeyed with no objection. Doug then headed to get the car as Alisha wrapped her daughter in a blanket and started toward the garage. Chloe said she needed to stop at the bathroom first and her mother went in with her. When they came out Salli was waiting by the door.

"Mom, can Salli come with us?"

"No Sweetie, she has to stay here."

"But Mom, I want her with me."

Alisha looked at Doug, who'd returned after moving the car to the driveway.

Doug responded, "I think it will be alright if she goes with us."

"What about when we get to the hospital? They won't let her in there."

"Then we will leave her in the car, but Chloe wants her with her now, it'll be alright."

"OK, let's just go."

So the entire family headed to the emergency room. During the drive, Alisha held Chloe on her lap; Robbie and Salli rode in the back. But for the entire ride Salli sat straight up, looking between the front seats at Chloe, who simply smiled at the dog with an occasional wave.

When they arrived at the hospital, Alisha quickly carried Chloe into the emergency room. While she managed the check-in process, Doug was on his way with Robbie, holding his son's hand. Unbeknownst to him, Salli had snuck out of the car with them and was also headed through the doors to reception when the security guard said, "Sorry sir, no dogs allowed."

Doug was startled to see Salli and stopped her before she could get fully through the door. "Sorry. She really wants to be with my daughter."

"Can't allow it, sir, I'm sorry. Rules, you understand."

"Sure. Robbie, go with Mom while I put Salli in the car."

Doug reached down to take Salli by the collar, but she pulled away and gave Doug that deep penetrating stare.

"Salli, dammit, I don't have time for this." He grabbed the dog's collar and tried to pull her back to the car, but she stood fast. Doug was pulled off balance and tried to pull harder but she locked her legs and body. Doug looked back at her and that stare. He understood. "You're not going to move, are you?" He looked over at the watching security guard. "Couldn't she just sit here, so she can see my daughter?"

"I...guess so. But if she gets in the way I will have to remove her, and quite frankly she doesn't look like she would be willing to do that."

"I don't think she'll cause any problems but you can always come get me if you need." With that, Doug led a more compliant Salli over to a window where she could see without blocking the entrance doors.

"You stay," instructed Doug, then hurried off to be with his family, being sure to seat them in a spot where the dog could see them. Salli sat still, watching attentively and giving Chloe a tail wag whenever the girl waved happily at her.

Finally a nurse came out and announced Chloe's name. Alisha went back with her while Doug stayed with Robbie. Salli was on her feet, on alert, where Doug had left her. He headed over and opened the door just enough to say, "It's OK. You stay, it's OK."

And Salli sat back down and quietly continued to keep watch.

After what seemed an eternity, Doug and Alisha heard the doctor's prognosis. She explained that seizures can be caused by numerous things and that they'd run tests to determine exactly what had happened. She also prescribed some muscle relaxers to help prevent any more seizures. Doug asked the doctor if she thought it was epilepsy. It was too early to tell, the doctor said, but assured them the tests would answer that question. Their family doctor would be contacted with the results in a few days, she promised, to share the results.

Doug and Alisha thanked the doctor and got up to head home. As they approached the exit doors, there stood Salli, wagging her tail furiously and panting with what could only be said was a dog's smile. She was clearly happy to see everyone, but especially Chloe. The two of them hugged and Chloe received a number of sloppy kisses.

As everyone headed toward the car the security guard followed, saying to Doug, "Sir, I gotta tell you about your dog." Doug braced for a haranguing that didn't come. "Not only did she not give me problems," the man said, "but while you were talking to the doctor an elderly couple came in and the man was helping his wife walk. I was on the phone so couldn't help as he struggled with the door, but you won't believe it. Your dog pushed the door open with his head and held it wide enough for them to enter. Afterward she returned to her post and waited for you guys to come out. That's one of the damnedest things I have ever seen."

CHAPTER 6

Once they were home again and got the kids back to bed, Doug and Alisha sat down on the couch and talked about Chloe.

Naturally they were worried, but both realized that until they got the test results there was nothing they could do. Eventually the conversation turned to Doug telling Alisha the story about Salli that the ER guard had told him. She thought about it for a few minutes before asking, "And how did she know what was happening to Chloe from the beginning? I believe she knew within seconds. With the door was closed and the TV on, I don't think we would have heard anything. So how did Salli know?"

"I don't know. I have heard of dogs being able to somehow sense when something's wrong. Whatever that is, it looks as if Salli has that ability. Because you're right, she had to have sensed it, rather than heard it."

"Well, it was amazing." She stroked Salli's head and neck and the dog responded by laying her head on Alisha's lap. Doug looked at the two of them and thought to himself, *"Exceptional. Maybe Jennifer was more correct than she knew."*

*****

The family doctor called a few days later. Epilepsy was not indicated in any of the test results; the conclusion was rather that the seizure had been caused by diuresis. It wasn't a serious condition but would need to be managed through diet and medications. Doug and Alisha were surprised to find Salli become a third committed participant to the new routine. One night when everyone was in the living room watching TV, Salli suddenly jerked to attention, hurried over to Chloe, began barking, and climbed into her lap. Then she barked at Doug and Alisha, who realized it was past time to give Chloe her medicine. Sure enough, Chloe had a slight seizure, and everyone agreed Salli was the reason it hadn't been more serious. They couldn't help but admit that the dog could somehow sense when a seizure was imminent. They marveled at this special talent, but had no idea what it would mean for their future.

CHAPTER 7

Around this time, Ray Allan moved to Oregon from Nevada to put down new roots, at least for the time being. Salem, a smallish, laid-back city, was perfect for him, even though he was used to a fast-track life. That's because Ray Allan was a grifter.

In his mid-thirties, handsome, and magnetic, Ray's MO was to combine a heart-melting smile with a pitiful hard-luck tale to win the hearts of troubled or needy women. He would charm his way into an invitation to live with them, proceed to bilk them and their families for as much money as possible, and then move on to another town. In each of the four previous grifts he'd pulled off successfully over the last decade or so, he'd netted more than $250K, not to mention all the free meals and lodging provided by the enamored and unsuspecting victims.

But Ray hadn't always been so successful with his scheme. About three years earlier he charmed a woman who it turned out wasn't as susceptible to his scam as the others. More than that, she set an elaborate trap to catch him red-handed. When the truth finally dawned on him that she had the gall to try to scam the scam artist herself, Ray Allan graduated from grifter to murderer in the blink of an eye.

Before the woman was able to communicate any of the information she'd weaseled out of him, Ray bludgeoned her to death in her own backyard, drove her body to a distant wooded area, and buried her deep in the ground in a place where a rock formation would conceal the spot from any unlikely passersby. He counted the ultimate outcome as a complete success, but the event had triggered something in his psyche that he'd never recognized before: Violence and physical cruelty made him feel good. He felt accomplished, all-powerful, and energized...even sexually, it enhanced his pleasure.

Now newly arrived in Salem, Ray met and set his sights on an attractive widow with a 7-year-old son. She worked for Ricoh's women's clothing so didn't make a ton of money, but carried no debt. It sure didn't hurt that she was also dynamite in bed. Plus, she had a wealthy sister and a brother who owned his own business, healthy one at that, grossing over $14K a month! Ray was sold, and doubled down to ensure another lucrative, delectable, success.

CHAPTER 8

By the time Salli reached her first birthday she had also reached 80 pounds. She sported a wide, muscular chest and neck, which tapering down to a slim stomach backed by powerful hind legs. Doug attributed a lot of her physique to the rigorous diet and training routine training he'd kept up, knowing it would calm anyone frightened by the sight of a Pit Bull to be assured at a glance how well-loved and well-trained she was. Salli had an extremely strong bite pressure and was amazingly fast and dexterous. Robbie once dropped a jar of peanut butter on his bare foot, releasing a scream of pain that startled everyone in the house. Doug leapt up to help, but even though he made it to the kitchen in a second, Salli was already there, licking Robbie's poor foot. No matter how quickly Doug ever reacted to something, his response time paled in comparison to Salli's.

It pained Doug to noticed, though, that their neighbors didn't accept Salli or feel safe around her. Even though she had only ever expressed behavior that was friendly and playful, people couldn't get past her stature and their prejudices against the breed. At the last neighborhood HOA meeting, the subject of Salli had even come up for discussion.

Some people wanted something said to Doug and Alisha about the dog in general to keep them on their guard. Others felt the HOAs should be changed to ban Pit Bulls from the partially gated neighborhood altogether. The discussion ended when someone pointed out that the dog had never done anything wrong, and warned the board that excluding one breed of dog could start a huge battle. The board tabled the discussion till the next meeting and suggested that people return having informed themselves a bit more about all aspects of the situation. Doug was equipped with information to try and calm more fears at the next meeting, but as fate would have it, Salli solved the problem for him.

*****

With Christmas just around the corner, Doug was busy putting up the family display of outdoor lights, with Salli as his *helper* while Alisha and the kids were out shopping. Salli wasn't leashed, since Doug knew she wouldn't wander off or disobey any of his commands, even if she roamed into the empty lot next to their house.

Doug was immersed in his work untangling a string of lights when through his peripherals he saw a small girl walking toward his house. The sweet 5-or-6-year-old was carrying an armful of Christmas packages. Doug heard a couple on the other side of the street wish her "Merry Christmas" and smiled, returning his concentration to the tangle of lights.

Suddenly a scream pierced through Doug, coming from where he'd seen the little girl. The couple on the other side of the street was screaming too. Doug jerked his head up and went cold at the sight of a Rottweiler clutching the child in its jaws.

Hurling the now-meaningless wires to the ground, Doug ran toward the girl. He could see in a blur the sight of the man across the street sprinting too. But of course Salli, as Doug had come to almost expect, had responded more quickly. Just before Doug set off toward the child, he'd heard in his bones Salli's guttural growl. But by the time his excited brain had released his body into a full run, his fiercely protective hound was already sprinting full-on toward the Rottweiler.

Startled by the oncoming force, the Rottweiler released its grip on the child. But that couldn't stop the Pit Bull from hitting the Rotty at full speed open jaws clamping down on the offending dog's vulnerable ear. Salli slammed into the Rotty so hard that together they tumbled top-over-tail, twice. All the while, Salli never released her bite.

When the pair finally tumbled to a stop, Salli kept her wits about her well enough to complete her gambit: Clamping down with her teeth, she tore off the Rotty's ear, with most of the face and neck skin coming with it. After a few squeals of pain and a failed attempt to escape, the Rottweiler fell silent.

Just then, Doug and the bystander couple caught up to the bloody scene, throwing their arms around the traumatized little girl. Doug was decisive about how to care for her: "Let's get her in to my house, investigate her injuries, and call an ambulance if necessary."

The woman exhorted to the little girl: "Honey, where do you live? Are your Mom or Dad around?"

The question was answered immediately by a frantic street-level scream from a woman who was clearly the girl's mother now at a full run herself. Arriving in a heave of last breath, she knelt down by her daughter, gutted by the sight of the torn skin and blood.

"What the hell happened?" she cried.

The bystander woman chimed in: "She was attacked by a dog."

The mom exploded in return: "I knew that goddamn Pit Bull was trouble! I knew it!"

Through all this, Doug had kept his gaze fixed on Salli, while all others were concentrating on the child he knew to be safe.

Now he put his hand on Salli's taut shoulder and said to the distraught parent: "No. Please believe me, Salli's the opposite of trouble. It's probable you can thank this Pit Bull for saving your daughter's life." After a pause confused by confused looks all around, he emphasized: "I mean it."

Amid all this the male bystander never stopped looking at Doug. Now he nodded soberly toward Salli and said, "Look at her. As soon as there was no fight left in the Rottweiler, she went on guard for the child and has not stopped. She's just watching and patrolling the entire area." He paused, gazing in confused awe at the scene he'd only too fully experienced or so he thought.

The bystander woman gawped at Doug too: "Is the dog trained to do that?"

Doug had to shake his head. "Not really." He felt so stunned by the situation that the random bystander started to became less random.

"I'm Jim Hollins. You're Doug, aren't you?"

"Yes."

"We met a couple times out taking walks."

"Oh? Yeah, I remember now. Sorry, I'm not thinking too straight."

"That's OK, totally understandable. Here's my business card. Call me as a witness if you need to."

"Witness?"

"I think your dog may have killed the other one. You just never know what might happen. It's better to be safe in case someone wants to try and sue. Ever seen that Rotty before?"

"Well no, now that you mention it."

"Got it. Well, to be safe I'm going to call the cops. They should come out and see this firsthand. Here's my word to you: I will support you and your dog to the fullest."

"Yea, huh. I guess cops would be a good idea. I hadn't had the clarity to think of it yet. Thanks, Jim. Thanks for the help."

"No Problem. To be honest, I'm impressed by what your dog did. And I don't want anything bad to happen. Do you get my meaning?"

Doug wasn't sure of anything at this moment. He wandered toward the two women who'd been comforting the girl and dressing her wound, asking the mother, "Can I call someone, maybe your husband?"

"It's just me."

"Then let me drive you to the emergency room."

Jim was right there to assist: "I'll handle the cops when they get here. She looks like she will be fine, Doug, but you should get her to the emergency room just to be safe."

The child's mother looked up and nodded, wrapped the little girl up into her arms and started to walk towards Doug's house. Suddenly Salli was at her side, scanning left to right for any other trouble. The mother looked down at the dog and started to say something, but stopped, instead turning a quizzical look to Doug.

"She's making sure that you and your daughter are protected."

The mother stopped still and watched as Salli also stopped, scanning the area while she waited for the mother's next move. In time the woman slowly started moving again, with Salli obediently shadowing her steps.

Doug acted fast, darting into the house to open the garage door. He quickly started the car and backed it out. He then got out, opened the passenger door and escorted in the mother, who bundled her sobbing daughter in her arms. As

Doug moved to quickly climb behind the wheel, he found Salli blocking his door, making it clear she wanted to get in.

"No Sal, you stay." He looked at the mother and said, "I have to put her in the house, I'll be right back."

"No, let her come."

"Oh no, I'll just be a second."

"No, really it's OK. I don't know why, but, I want her to come."

Doug looked at her for a few seconds. He then got out and opened the back door and Salli jumped in. As they drove to the hospital Salli sat on the floor of the back seat with her head resting lightly on the legs of the little girl. The girl no longer cried; her hand was rested against Salli's snout.

When they arrived at the hospital, the mother got out and quickly moved toward the emergency room entrance with her daughter in hand. Doug followed but quickly realized that Salli was walking alongside him. As they reached the ER doors Doug said, "You have to stay here, girl." And just as if she understood she went to the window and started her vigil.

Doug explained the situation to the guard and

said he would be back in few minutes to put the dog in the car. The guard reluctantly agreed. Doug went in the waiting room and sat next to the mother and daughter he'd become an unexpected guardian to.

"Everything go OK?"

The mother nodded her head. "She should be going in any second."

As if on cue, a nurse came out and said, "Amy McClain?"

Amy stood with her daughter and walked toward the ER. Doug said, "I'll wait outside with the dog, but I'll watch for you." The mother turned, nodded and smiled, saying, "Thank you."

A feeling of Déjà vu came over Doug as he emerged to where Salli was sitting just outside the ER doors. It was just as she'd been with Chloe. He moved to the car and waited, still feeling the déjà vu creeping through him. When Salli bolted for the doors, Doug knew Amy and her daughter had come out and headed over to check on them.

Salli vigorously wagged her tail as she walked alongside the mother carrying her daughter.

"How'd it go?" Doug inquired.

"Fine, they patched her up and gave her a tetanus shot. No major arteries were damaged. She has to go see our doctor tomorrow. They also want to know about the dog that attacked her."

Doug remembered Jim's card. He called and when Jim answered he got the scoop on the police visit. The Rottweiler had not died at the scene and the police took him to a vet. After some tests and information gathering, the dog was put to sleep. A rabies test was being performed as they spoke. Both Doug and Amy would have to file reports with the police. Doug explained the situation to Amy as he drove her home.

When they arrived, Amy asked Doug and Salli to come in for a few minutes. Doug agreed and followed her into the house. Once she had closed the door, she set her daughter on the floor. Salli cautiously approached the little girl, and when the child smiled and moved in close, Salli licked her on the arm. The girl smiled and hugged Salli around the head. The wagging tail picked up speed with the contact.

Amy smiled and said, "Somehow she feels safe around your dog. Amazing after what just happened."

"Yea, I get that. Salli has the ability to sense things that I really don't understand."

"Well it sure is working on Maddie. That's my daughter's name, Maddie. Short for Madeline.

And I'm Amy, Amy McClain."

"I'm Doug Thomas and that's Salli, Salli with an i."

Amy looked at him with a slight smile. He shook his head, grinned and said, "Long story."

She offered coffee and Doug accepted. They talked for over an hour while Maddie and Salli played. Finally Doug said it was time to go. Amy said, "Thank you so much. You guys were our heroes and we won't ever forget that. And Salli, I'm very sorry for thinking you were the bad dog."

"It was our pleasure," Doug returned.

Amy hugged Doug, kissed his cheek and looked into his eyes. "Maybe we can see each other again."

"We probably will, seeing we're in the same neighborhood." He smiled back at her.

"Then it's a date."

Doug's gazed hitched up for a slight moment before he said, "Sure." He looked at Maddie as she hugged Salli hard around the neck. Salli seemed elated with the affection as she licked a big kiss on Maddie's face, sending Maddie into delightful giggles.

After Doug got in his car he sat for a moment reflecting about the exchange he'd had with Amy. Still a bit befuddled by the randomness, he eventually shook his head and drove home. Once there, Alisha asked where he had been and he told her the whole story. Except about the goodbye from Amy, which he hadn't made sense of himself.

*****

The police came by the next day and Doug told the story again. In the end, though, nothing came of it. The police eventually found the owner of the Rottweiler, but the dog had just escaped, no surprise to anyone considering the deplorable conditions the dog had been kept in by an owner who didn't have sufficient money to feed the beast.

CHAPTER 9

Melissa sat looking at the phone. She was sure that Doug would be happy for her, but he was her big brother and big brothers can get a little weird. She remembered what he did the time her ex-husband Danny grabbed her arm when they were in Doug's house. At that time everyone knew Danny was cheating on her. They also knew he was making her life miserable, and that he was abusive.

Melissa had said something that made Danny mad and he instinctively and mistakenly grabbed her arm in anger. Doug didn't hesitate. The hate he had for this man who was maligning his sister came to a head instantly. He threw a right-hand punch directly into Danny's face, leaving him stumbling to the floor surprised by the blood flowing out from the cut under his right eye. Danny immediately rose from the floor and threatened a lawsuit, to which Doug replied, "Go for it. Then everyone will know what an asshole you really are!"

Danny left Melissa and James sometime later

and never darkened their door again. Melissa got their son, and a onetime payment of $15,000. She knew he would never make monthly payments, so she accepted the lump sum as the end of everything between them. She put it into a savings account and kept it there in case of emergency.

Now here she was eleven months later, about to tell Doug that there was someone new in her life. Someone her brother didn't know, someone frankly she didn't really know, yet. She knew he was from Las Vegas and that he was some type of financial consultant. She also was well aware that he was good-looking, charming and treated her like a princess. Also, for the first time in many years, or possibly ever, he effectuated her sexual desire. That was something she wanted to know a lot more about indeed.

She took a deep breath and picked up the phone and dialed Doug's number.

"Hiya, Sis!"

"Hi, Dougie."

"Dougie?! Uh oh, you must want something."

It was true that when they were younger she called him Dougie whenever she wanted him to do her a "big brother" favor. "Ha, no, I don't want anything, you big jerk. I just called to tell you...

that...I, uh..."

"Sis, it's me. Just spit it out."

"I've met someone. I was having lunch one day at the little café just down from my store. And we just kinda met and he asked me out. We've been seeing each other for about a month now."

"Really...that's great, Sis. He a good guy?"

She felt a silent flare of unexpected anger at such a typical response from him. She knew how he thought: Her track record rendered her completely incapable of making good choices. Infuriating.

Melissa had been with just one other guy since Danny. It's true he turned out to be a nasty little jerk with an ego so large it blocked out the sun for anyone around him. That's exactly why Melissa had ended it after no more than 6 weeks. But this was different. She'd finally found someone who was nice to her, who treated her well. And Doug was going to find fault with that?

Aware of the awkward pause, she started to reply, just as Doug was realizing his gaffe. "I'm sorry Sis. That sounded condescending as hell and I didn't mean it to come across like that. I just worry about you and that makes me say stupid things sometimes. Forgive me?"

Sweet relief! "Sure, thanks Doug. I know you

worry, and I'm the first to admit I've made a few poor choices over the years, but this guy is absolutely wonderful. He treats me great and respects me for who I am. I can't remember when I was last treated this good, Doug. I love it, and I think this guy is the real deal."

"OK, sorry I sounded overprotective." He warmed into the role of supportive older sibling. "Tell me about him."

"Well, he's a couple years older than I am, but aging beautifully, he's quite the looker. More important, he's polite and really treats me well—he's great to me, really, I just can't believe it!"

"What does he do?"

"He's an independent financial consultant."

Doug winced a bit but kept his mouth shut. He was not a fan of financial investors and being a "consultant" sounded like a shady way to snatch people's money any which way but loose. Still he took the supportive high ground: "Sounds great, Sis. Let us know a time we can get together and meet him. Does he live around here?"

"Well, right now, he's...staying with me. Temporarily. Till he finds a place of his own to live."

Doug's cool veneer burnt away instantly. "He's *living* with you!"

"Just for now."

She heard Doug sigh, but then say, "Ok. Be careful, Sis, and believe me, I mean that in the nicest possible way."

"I know, Doug. I promise I will be careful. I love you."

"Love you too." The called ended and Doug ran his fingers through his hair. He didn't like the sound of this, but hey, she's a grown woman and surely she can spot a jerk, especially after all she's learned from the previous ones. He swallowed his concern and went back to work.

CHAPTER 10

The kid stood stock still in the back yard for a full minute, watching the house. Then he slowly crept toward the kitchen window. Carefully, he removed the screen and pulled the sliding frame to the right, standing on a lawn chair he had liberated from the patio. He slowly and silently lifted the blinds, checked thoroughly that no one was inside, stayed completely silent and observant for another full minute to be sure there was zero human activity, and then quietly stepped through the open window.

Doug and Alisha had gone to bed around 11PM and both were sound asleep. Salli was in her normal position, sprawled on the end of the bed centered between Doug and Alisha. Now, around 2 AM, she suddenly and silently lifted her head, listening intently. Almost immediately she jumped off the bed and padded out the door into the hallway. Listening again, she stood silent for a minute before continuing toward the kitchen.

By now the kid had maneuvered his whole body inside the house. From his intruder perch in the sink, he surveyed the room, grateful for a night light that illuminated the immediate surroundings. When he was sure there was no activity happening, he began to hoist himself down to the floor.

Salli entered the kitchen at that moment, propelled cautiously by the sense that something was not normal. As soon as she rounded the kitchen island she encountered the kid, just as he planted both his feet on the floor. He pivoted his frame toward the room, catching sight of Salli, whose taut canine frame was backed against the counter, her eyes fixed on him-- staring intently. Paralyzed by fear, he could only stare back. Neither moved for a full twenty seconds.

The kid's mind raced, even as he tried to remain motionless. What the hell do you do, faced with an 80lb pit bull staring at you in the near-dark of a house you don't belong in.

"Maybe if I could get on the counter and over to the window quick enough, that dog wouldn't be able to get me," his addled brain suggested. But his face frowned in return; he shook his head. *"That thinking is crap! That dog is no more than 3 feet from you. Try to bolt and the beast will jerk you off the counter as quick as Chopper sics balls in "Stand By Me" and will swallow you (and your balls) whole. Think, damnit!"*

The clichés from that and so many other movies

didn't seem so far-fetched, all of a sudden. Thank god his buddy had encouraged him to carry dog treats just in case—as he suddenly recalled amid the terror. He jerked his hand into his pocket and proffered a lint-covered treat gingerly toward the dog's vice-like snout.

He whispered, "Here puppy, take the nice treat, yum, it's really good."

Salli wasn't having it. She never flinched, nor even acknowledged the treat. She simply continued her stare, refusing to avert her eyes from the interloper's.

"Oh, that's just great!" The kid whispered to himself. *"10 billon dogs in the world and I rob the house of the one that doesn't like treats."* But still, he thought, possibly I could slink to the right of the kitchen island and maybe inch my way to the front door, and escape. He slowly started to walk to the right.

Salli wasn't having it. She instantly moved around the island and blocked the thief's path to the right, making no sounds or moves toward the invader. This was somehow even more disconcerting to the increasingly nervous kid.

Weighing odds, he backed up to roughly the same spot he'd been in before. Salli, seeming like a canine chess master, positioned herself so that she had both paths around the island blocked.

Again their eyes met.

The kid whispered in angry confusion, "What the hell am I supposed to do now? You know, you act like you're giving me a chance to re-think this. Is that it? You giving me a chance?" He continued his gaze into her eyes. "Maybe you are? OK, I'll bite."

The thief smiled nervously at his unconscious word choice, lifted both hands, and tried to lighten the mood: "Just a figure of speech," he smiled.

He moved deliberately, never taking his eyes off the dog he didn't know as Salli, but knew to respect and fear. With his back against the counter, he placed the palms of his hands on the top and rose his feet off the ground until he could sit. He spun his legs toward the sink and put both feet in. He then scooted his butt along the counter until he was able to slowly raise his body up toward the open window. Through all this choreography, he never took his eyes off the dog.

Still on edge, he protruded his feet out the window, then turned stomach-down to slide out. When he felt the lawn chair he looked up, only to encounter the strange dog's penetrating eyes.
She had positioned herself with her front paws on the counter, her hind legs still on the floor. They locked stares. The stranger nodded soberly, whispering, *"Promise."* He completed

his befuddled and worshipful release from the place he'd so recently thought he could master. Closing the window, he left everything the way it had been before he arrived.

Salli stayed at the kitchen window for few minutes, but then slowly made her way back to the bedroom and her spot on the bed. Doug and Alisha never knew a thing about the break in.

CHAPTER 11

The holidays had come and gone and spring was approaching quickly. Doug and Salli were out in the front yard. He was busy weeding and fertilizing in preparation for the growing season, while she watched intently, seemingly ready to offer help if ever the soil required it. This pattern generally unfolded with Doug having to ask her to shift out of his way every few minutes, but they were both basically ok with that and genuinely happy with the arrangement.

Suddenly Salli lifted her head and shot a look down the street. She instantly started wagging her tail as she recognized the two people walking toward the house. Doug followed the trajectory of her enthusiasm to spy the mother and daughter they'd met at the Rottweiler incident. Amy and Maddie were coming their way. When Maddie saw Salli she broke into a run to close the distance. She was enthusiastically met by an already-on-the-move Salli, who was more than willing to accept the hugs and affection that Maddie was dishing out. Doug smiled and walked over to where Amy was standing. "How are the two of you doing?" he asked.

"Actually, very well. Thanks for asking. Maddie seems to not have any residual effects from the dog attack. Thanks to you."

"Oh, not me, as much as it was Salli. I'm just glad it turned out as well as it did. "

"Me too. If you and Salli hadn't been in the yard that day, who knows what would have happened!"

"Well, I'm glad we were." He glanced again at the nuzzling girl and dog and said, "Salli sure likes her."

"And she sure likes Salli! Say, why don't you stop by the house some time for lunch or dinner? It's the least we could do to thank you." She slowly lifted her eyes, smiling sweetly, which pushed her bottom lip out into a slight pout. "You need to be thanked."

Doug found himself a bit flustered. "No thanks are necessary. But with spring coming, we will be out more and maybe we'll see each other."

Amy reached down and took his hand. As she lifted it up she slowly slid her thumb down between his knuckles and grazed the lengths of a couple fingers before letting go. She smiled and said, "I look forward to it." She gathered up Maddie and they walked on down the street.

She smiled to herself. She liked Doug and truly hoped he would come around sometime.

"Phew...what the hell was that Sal?" Doug looked at the dog. Doug had to admit to himself that the experience he just had, felt good. It was nice to know that someone like Amy found him attractive and interesting. He loved Alisha and loved their life, but as often happens after 20+ years of marriage, life had gotten in the way of intimacy. Bills and jobs had taken over for conversations and flirting. Television had become more important than the art of 'spur of the moment' actions. Sex had also become routine and predictable. So the fact that the attractions of a younger and beautiful woman had stirred some emotions in Doug wasn't completely out of the realm. He went back to digging in the flower bed deciding to keep this secret and not share it with Alisha.

Doug saw Amy a few times after that encounter while he walked with Salli and once in the grocery store. Amy was always flirtatious and asked about getting together, but nothing had happened.

CHAPTER 12

Summer had arrived and it was time for the annual Thomas family reunion. It had become a tradition for Doug and Alisha to host a BBQ for their entire family around July 4th every year. This year, everyone was able to come, which meant a sizeable crowd to feed and entertain.

Alisha's mother and father would be there along with her brother Allen and of course Jennifer and the two girls. Her sister Mary was able to arrange her schedule to attend, but was not bringing a date this year. Doug's mother was attending, which was a major development. Doug's father had died of cancer a few years earlier and his mother had become a bit of a recluse since. His sister Julianne and her husband Clark had somehow found a way to take time out of their busy schedules to join the reunion this year, and of course his sister Melissa and her son Jamey would be there. This was an especially highly anticipated gathering for Melissa, she'd chosen the occasion to introduce the family to the new man in her life, Ray Allan.

That made for 17 people scheduled to attend, including Doug, Alisha and their two kids. Which made for a lot of planning, cleaning, and stress. Doug and Alisha got it all done, but at a cost that saw them barely speaking to each other on the event day. But as people starting arriving, no one would have guessed there was any strife between the two of them. Everyone was greeted cheerfully with hugs and kisses and whatever beverage they wanted. As everyone talked and laughed, Doug prepared the BBQ with hot dogs, hamburgers, ribs and corn on the cob. Alisha busily prepared the salads, beans, condiments and kept everyone stocked with their favorite beverage. Good times were being had by all.

When Melissa, Jamey and Ray Allan arrived, everyone was certainly interested in the new man in her life. Ray was winding his way through crowd, externally pouring on the charm with the entire family. Internally he was analyzing each person's weaknesses and strengths, as you'd expect from a natural born scam artist—but the family had no reason to suspect.

It was a well-worn instinct for Ray to read people and gain potentially useful information from them, all the while making an appealing impression on everyone. He was easily perceived to be a wonderful and amiable guest. All the family members took to him immediately and felt that Melissa had picked a winner.

Only Ray knew the truth: that he was anything but wonderful. He was a hardened criminal with little or no remaining conscience. His plan for this chapter of the adventure he took life to be, was to set up a retirement account for Melissa and Jamey. He would convince her to put in all she could to build toward her and her son's future. Of course he offered up his phony investment service as a great way to invest for all the family. His partner in Las Vegas would ensure the business looked like a profitable and wise financial choice.

Then, when Melissa, and others, had invested enough money, she'd find Ray simply gone one day—along with all the preciously saved money. This was all very "rinse and repeat" for our scammer Ray. He had it down to a science.

Living with the target was key to his success. It was important for her to be easily manipulated while offering a pleasing environment for Ray to operate in. He loathed playing the necessary role of doting boyfriend eager to be part of the family, so to make it palatable to his method, he at least wanted a target who would please his every wish. So far Melissa had fit the bill perfectly this go-round.

In this first meeting with her family, he'd made a few foundational assessments. Doug's sister

Julianne was elegant, caring and exceedingly friendly—and naive. Her husband Clark, though, a banking bigwig, was going to be a problem. He was smart, rich and savvy. With his financial industry savvy, he might see through Ray's scheme and potentially screw up the whole plan.

Allen and Jennifer were basically stupid. Their lives revolved around their two snot-nosed kids. They'd definitely never be good marks for Ray, since they never thought beyond the next paycheck.

But Ray intuited interesting possibilities with Alisha's sister, Mary. She was a divorced airline attendant who wasn't dating anyone at the moment—all good indicators of someone with money who knew she needed to invest in her future. A little persuasion by the charming Ray could pay dividends.

Doug's mother appeared to be a total bust. It didn't appear that she had much money and she was in a vegetable state after the loss of her dear sweet husband, who probably was also a total loser, if you could tell by the sad widow's wardrobe and jewelry.

Alisha's mother and father also fell smack dab into the stupid category. It was plain to see where Allen had inherited his stupidity. Close to retirement, they would be virtually impossible to bilk out of any money; he instantly wrote off the pair off as a waste of his valuable time.

Doug and Alisha, however, were different from the rest of their clan. Ray sensed problems there, or at least current bad times. There was some tension between them that, depending on how it panned out, could be very good for Ray. Alisha was sweet, caring and trusting. Doug represented a bit more risk—seeming strong, decisive and future-focused—but depending on how tensions might evolve between them, Alisha could make them an easier mark as a pair.

Having made his seemingly pleasant rounds, Ray felt cocky about his assessment of the Thomas family. His outlook was good. He may have to eliminate good ol' Banker Clarkie, but that was no problem; in fact that might be kinda fun, and —if things went right—could be a very lucrative venture in itself.

Ray smirked at the possibilities splayed before him. His body glowed with overwhelming satisfaction, brought on by the mere *thought* of ruining this family. He felt himself getting hard and smiled at Melissa, who lovingly returned the smile. He drew a deep breath and envisioned what he could bring the late night to hold.

While Ray reveled in his own hubris, the family member he had forgotten about watched his every move.

CHAPTER 13

The family reunion was winding down as the sun set and the back yard was getting dark. The house was backed by a golf course, and the sunset cast a reddish glow over much of the back yard and the fairway that flanked it. The men helped with cleanup, then sat on the patio smoking cigars and drinking bourbon or scotch. The girls were in the kitchen half-heartily cleaning up, but whole-heartily consuming wine while telling stories and laughing.

The three older children were engrossed in their game and having fun. They each had assumed different characters and were busily enhancing their persona with new equipment and conquering new levels in the enchanted land where the game took place. The two younger kids were playing with action figures and dolls. Jennifer occasionally went to the door of the back bedroom where the kids were playing and listened. When satisfied with the voices she heard, Jennifer returned to the kitchen to join in the other fun. Alisha had put Salli behind closed doors in their bedroom, since she didn't seem to know which way to go whenever there were a lot of people around in different places. In these instances, Alisha found that it was easier on everyone to put her in a different room.

At some time, the two younger girls became bored with the dolls and decided to go on a real adventure outside. It was still light enough to see, so they exited the house through the front door without anyone noticing. The three older kids, engrossed in their own world, hadn't noticed the departure.

Candice, who was now 5 years old and the leader of her crew of two, held Kathleen's hand as they headed left down the fairway in the back of the house. Going left meant shielding their view from the sight of the adults, so they strolled without concern of being noticed. They were headed toward a wooded area about a quarter mile from the house.

There, a stream ran through the back part of the golf course. The banks of the stream were approximately 5 feet high, covered in tall grass and other vegetation. The male golfers always used it as a 'relief station', but for a 5-year and 3-year-old, it was an adventure waiting to happen.

The creek itself was overgrown with blackberries and other shrubs and was a known home for coyotes that lived on the golf course. The girls arrived just as it was getting dark. They curiously sauntered to the creek and walked along the side peering down at the babbling water.

They were particularly excited when they saw the rare unsettling creature called a Nutria sitting near the bank. They moved closer to get a better view of the creature sitting under the extended and overgrown branches surrounded by blackberry vines. They both giggled in delight at the sight of the creature sitting on its haunches while holding a twig in its front paws and delightfully munching away. Upon hearing the giggles, the Nutria retreated further under the extended branch.

As you can imagine, the girls then needed to adjust their position to continue watching. After moving closer, and just as Candice stepped to a spot where they could see better, the ground unexpectedly gave out and they both tumbled toward the creek.

Candice, holding her sister's hand tightly, somehow pulled Kathleen over her head and she crashed down onto the extended limb. It was all unexpected, to say the least!

Sadly, all this activity left the younger sister pinned between the overgrown branches and blackberry vines -- her legs dangling over the water. Candice had crashed violently head-first into the water, and knocked herself unconscious on a rock, hitting in such a way to render her body limp. Candace rolled onto her back from the cold strange solace of the rushing water. Kathleen was still conscience, her chest wedged between the branches, cutting off her breathing. She cried and screamed but it was barely audible. The coyote pack immediately took notice and cautiously pranced off to investigate.

*****

Just as the two girls had started their trek to the stream, Salli jerked awake from sleep, in her familiar position on the end of the bed. She walked to the front of the bed and tried to look out the window, but the lowered blinds prevented her from seeing. She got down off the bed and proceeded to pace back and forth, occasionally stopping and tilting her head, processing incoming data.

She whined the whole time and scratched at the door to be let out. No one was around to hear her as the party continued. As the two girls approached the creek, Salli now sat down close to the window and stared at the closed blinds. The pacing and whining had stopped. Now in its place was total concentration. Every fiber in her muscular body focused solely on the girls. She tilted her head at the exact second the ground gave out. She then charged the bedroom double doors and slammed her body into them. She began loudly barking in an urgent chorus and continued the banging on the door. It took only seconds for Alisha to run to the doors and open them.

Salli burst out of the room and ran to the kitchen and the backdoor. Doug had jumped up and opened the back door and as Salli ran to the open door, he quickly closed it.

"What the hell is going on?!" Salli now started barking loudly and urgently at Doug, but he didn't open the door. So she quickly ran to the hallway and barked again while making a motion of going down the hallway. Doug realized that Salli was telling him to follow. By now the older children had opened their bedroom door and Salli ran in the open door and began barking at the empty space where the girls had been playing. Doug said, "The girls! Jennifer, your two girls are gone! See if we can find them!"

Now Salli headed to the back door and began barking again. She never looked around, just stared at the closed door. Everyone was frantically running through the house screaming the girl's names and looking in rooms, under beds, and closets. Doug finally looked at Salli and said: "She knows something."

He ran to the back door and opened it. Like a bullet fired from a high-powered rifle, Salli raced down the fairway into the darkening night. She knew exactly where she was going.

*****

By now the coyotes had sufficiently scouted the area. They closely watched the two girls and their surroundings. But before making a move to cash in on this unexpected feast, they carefully made sure there was no danger.

The male circled the area, winding his way to about 5 feet from the unconscious Candice. Slowly and cautiously he approached her still body, which lay half in the water and half out. Carefully observing the surroundings, he bared his teeth, opened his mouth and lunged at her bare legs lying on the dry ground.

But his teeth never touched flesh.

In that moment, as if the whole scene had played out in advance in Salli's canine mind, she hurtled through the air toward the coyote, making crucial contact a mere instant before the beast could make contact with Candice. In one violent motion, Salli bit down on the coyote's neck, snapping it like a dry branch. She gave one instinctive shake and dropped the coyote dead before moving toward the girls.

On the run, Salli grabbed Candice's shirt in her mouth, delicately pulling her out of the water. Licking her face and nudging her chest, she then began a loud and constant barking to signal the following rescuers.

She then located Kathleen and somehow managed to tear through the blackberry vines to get up on the branch next to her. But instantly she was forced to stop her barking, changing her register to warn the other coyotes with a growl and snarl that sounded straight out of a werewolf movie.

The other coyotes left immediately -- no hesitation. Salli accessed the situation and quickly determined that she could not help, except to comfort. She began her steady signal barking again, sans the occasional lick to Kathleen's face and watchful eye over Candice.

Doug and Allen arrived on the scene first, followed by Clark and Ray, all wielding flashlights. Allen descended the bank and went to Candice. He started frantically crying and screaming for her to wake up. Clark jumped down next to him and checked for a heartbeat.

He calmed Allen and said: "She's not dead. She has a heartbeat and it sounds strong. Let's get her back to the house and to hospital."

Allen then realized that he had not seen Kathleen and started hysterically screaming for her.

Doug started looking with the flashlight to spot her.

Salli then began barking with an excited pitch

and Doug knew instantly that she was with Kathleen.

Ray Allan who was still top-side shined his flashlight toward the tree with the extended branches and yelled, "Here!"

Doug quickly moved to the branches, and located Kathleen with his beam of light.

"I see her! She's alive and Salli is with her. I'm going to get her out."

He quickly ascertained that he would not be able to get to her through the blackberry vines, so he yelled up to Ray. "Can I get to her from up there?"

Ray moved to the tree and peered down.

"Yes, there are some blackberry vines but should be able to get through. I can go."

Doug said, "No, I can get there quicker from here. He moved to and pushed his way up the trunk of the tree and shoved the vines away with his arm. The thorns painfully tore into his skin, but he didn't flinch and pushed forward. His legs straddled the branches and he moved toward Kathleen. That movement squeezed the branches together even more and Salli quickly noticed that Kathleen's breath was becoming shorter and more labored. She then pushed her front paws between the two branches and stopped them from further collapsing together. She then took the back of Kathleen's shirt in her mouth and lifted the little girl up and back, allowing her to breathe more freely. When Doug got to her, he saw what Salli was doing and had an instantaneous flash of amazement. It faded quickly as he set about freeing the girl from the branches. Once he had safely gotten her out, he handed her to Ray who quickly passed her to Allen. They all, including Salli, quickly returned home to the waiting family. An ambulance was called and within minutes the two girls were off to the hospital along with their family. The only ones to stay behind were Doug, Clark, Ray and Salli. The three older children stayed also but huddled together in the living room.

CHAPTER 14

On the patio with the lights on, Doug gingerly applied medication to the scratches and cuts from the blackberry vines. He also removed thorns and applied medication to Salli. She had plowed straight through the worst of the vines and had come out much worse in terms of cuts and buried thorns. Doug carefully worked on Salli and promised himself to take her into the Vet the next morning. Clark and Ray sat silently and watched. Finally Clark said, "Doug, there is a question screaming to be asked."

Doug looked at him, scowled slightly and then said, "What is it?"

"How the hell did that dog do that?"

"Do what?"

"Know exactly when, where and how all this took place. Christ Doug, she knew enough to tell you that the kids were missing, by actually taking you to the room and showing you! Then, when you opened the door and she came out, never hesitated, never sniffed the air and never even looked in a different direction. She ran full speed to exactly the spot where the girls were."

Doug was looking at Salli then lifted his eyes to Clark and said, "And, she knew what to do to save them."

"What do you mean?"

"When I went to get Kathleen off that branch, Salli was wedging herself between the two branches to relieve pressure off Kathleen's chest. She was *also* lifting her up with her mouth to keep her away from the pinching of the branches. And as you can see she went through hell to get to her. "

Ray Allan then spoke, "Did anyone else see the dead coyote?"

Both looked over at Ray, and shook their heads.

"He was just a few feet from where the girl was lying. I checked him and he was most certainly dead but he was still warm and fresh blood coming out of a wound in his neck. A bite wound. It had to have been your dog. So now you can add saving the girl's life from a wild animal."

The three men looked in total amazement at Salli, who lay calmly licking her wounds. Ray Allan thought, *I wonder if she is smart enough to fuck up my plans. Perhaps one more elimination may be needed. She could keep old Clarkie boy com-*

pany.

As those thoughts ran through his head, Salli suddenly stopped licking and stared at Ray. He didn't notice.

CHAPTER 15

The next morning Doug called and got an appointment with his vet. The appointment was for 1PM and when he arrived they were taken into a room immediately. The vet came in shortly and examined Salli. She gave her shots of antibiotics, a rabies booster and gave Doug some medicated cream to apply to her wounds for a few days. The vet assured Doug that her wounds did not appear serious. He told her about the dead coyote and then went into detail about the entire story, finishing by saying, "I don't know what to think. Do I have some kind of special dog?"

The vet looked over to Salli, then back at him and said, "It does sound bizarre. I am a firm believer in dogs' aptitude to sense and understand things, far more than humans give them credit for. Some are better than others, but what you described goes way beyond any instinctual characteristics I have ever witnessed or heard of."

"Should I do something?"

"Well, I know a dog psychologist."

"A what?"

The vet chuckled and said, "You heard me correctly, a dog psychologist. There are such things. They generally deal with behavior, but the guy I know might be interested in delving into this."

"Sounds expensive."

"Well, he's not cheap, but for this he might be open to see her for free just for the knowledge."

"Well, if it's free, I might take her in to see him, at least once," Doug said before heading home with his "wonder dog."

The vet immediately called her friend, the dog psychologist, who was indeed intrigued. He took down the contact information and set up a "gratis" appointment with Doug and Salli for the following Friday at 4PM.

*****

In preparation for the visit, the animal psychologist prepared a series of tests to give to Salli and a series of questions to ask Doug. At the appointed time, Doug and Salli walked into the office and were greeted at the door.

"Doug, I'm Dr. William Clark. It is nice to meet you and I am looking forward to getting to know more about your dog here." He looked down at

Salli and said, "She's a big one."

Doug smiled, "Yes she is. She tips the scales at a little over 80lbs. She has the look of a dangerous dog, but she's really a big sweetie."

"However," countered Dr. Clark, "based on the story your vet told me, she can become quite protective and subsequently violent when necessary. That is, when she feels that someone she cares about is in danger. Would you agree?"

"I guess that's fair. She seems to know when something bad is about to happen and prevents it, but even in those situations her aggression is limited to just the bad element. Then she snaps out of it very quickly and it seems, quite frankly, to abhor having to do anything violent."

He recounted the stories of Chloe and the neighbor girl Maddie, and finally the story of the two lost girls. Dr. Clark nodded and listened carefully throughout, and then said, "Hmm, seems she does have some unusual abilities. Why don't we run her through a few exercises I designed for her?" Doug nodded his approval and they set to work.

The activities were ostensibly evaluating Salli's behavior and in-the-moment instincts, but privately the doctor was also observing how she acted *between* the exercises. Were her senses heightened following each test? Did she seem to anticipate the doctor's next move as he proceeded through the exercises?

Before their arrival, Dr. Clark had also hidden a block of 2x4 wood about 6" long in the couch cushions. He purposely never said anything about the item's presence or gave any indication of its whereabouts. After talking over the test results with Doug, he casually looked over at Salli and said, "Well, weren't you a good girl today?" But as he said these words he made a point to form a (false) thought in his mind: *As soon as you two get up to leave, I'm going to get the block of wood in the cushions of the couch and bash Doug in the head with it.*

Afterward Dr. Clark walked them to the lobby and turned back toward his office. But before Doug and Salli closed much distance toward the exit, Salli turned, trotted back to the doctor's office, and jumped up on the couch while Dr. Clark looked on. She calmly retrieved the block of wood, dropped it at his feet, gave him a quick glance, and unceremoniously returned to Doug's side.

After they'd gone, Dr. Clark sat dumbstruck in his office chair, rubbing his temples with his fingers. Eventually he emitted a short sharp laugh. "Sonofabitch."

CHAPTER 16

The next day Dr. Clark called an associate in the Chicago area. This associate was renowned in the field of psychology, mainly with humans but dabbled some with animals. The doctor didn't quite know how he was going to explain what he had seen but he wanted to try. He dialed the number and when the office secretary answered the phone, he said, "May I speak with Alex please, this is Dr. William Clark."

"Of course sir, I will transfer you to his office." the secretary said, and immediately transferred the call to Dr. Alex Smythe.

"Will! Good to hear from you. Why am I being blessed with this call?"

"Hi Alex, well it's always good to talk with you, but truth be told, I have the goddamnest story to tell you that I ever thought possible."

"You've peaked my curiosity," Dr. Smythe replied, sitting back to listen as Dr. Clark told his story. Afterward, Dr. Smythe simply sat quietly and thought on what he had just heard.

"Alex, are you still there?" asked Will.

"Yes, I'm here. Frankly, I'm still trying to digest the tale you just told me. If all you said is true, and I do not doubt your veracity, then you may have an amazing find on your hands. A few questions, if I might?"

"Of course."

"Did you actually see the events described in the rescue story of the two girls?"

"No."

"Then we don't know for sure that it's completely accurate. I do not think, however, that the story would be too exaggerated, given the fact that no one is seeking fame or fortune. So my next questions are directed to you, Will. When you ran the tests at your office, did anyone have prior knowledge of the tests you were to conduct?"

"No, none whatsoever."

"And the dog showed perception abilities?"

"Absolutely, more so than any other canine I have ever tested. I would go so far as to say, amazing."

"And when you planted this 'wood weapon,' as you called it, no one saw you hide it?"

"No one, I was very careful to be sure. Not even my secretary."

"And at no time did you reveal your secret to the owner? Or look at the hidden spot, or even glance at it?"

"Not even the slightest shift in my eyes. Alex, I feel very strongly that this dog not only sensed where the weapon was, but she also knew I was bluffing about using it. And, the way she dropped the block of wood at my feet…she's got a sense of humor. This goes way beyond simple perception. This dog knew what I was thinking."

"Surely you don't believe that the dog read your mind? Will, if that is indeed what you're thinking, then I must insist you come back to earth. I do not believe of this ability in humans, let alone in animals. The very thought of an animal being able to understand the human tongue, but to even understand something that hasn't been spoken?"

"I don't know what to believe. I saw this with my own eyes and yes, it goes against all rationality, but… something is telling me that this dog is, I don't know…Extra-sensory."

"Then I should like to meet this dog and his owner. This is a very unusual case as you have explained it. I think further research would be an absolute must. Can you set up a time that I might fly out to you and we can together spend some time with this *special* animal?"

"I'll start the process and get back to you with some dates and possible ideas for further research. And, the dog is a she."

"Well, that explains a lot!" The two chuckled and hung up.

CHAPTER 17

Alisha, who worked part time at a local law office as a legal aide, was preparing for her work day.

As she dressed and applied her makeup, she thought of Doug. They had really never talked about the family BBQ from over a month ago, and there was still a lot of tension between them. She'd noticed that he had become very distant and would not engage in any discussions about their life or current situation. And just last night they'd had another argument that resulted in her going to bed early and Doug sleeping in the guest room.

She didn't know if he was having an affair or if he'd just become so busy with business, and his new dog, that he just didn't care anymore. The fire they'd kindled between themselves for so many years was seemingly fading to a dim, dying ember. She thought about the last time they had made love: quick, efficient and business-like, not at all as it'd been for so many years prior.

She thought of all the times they'd spent just

talking. This kind of daily connection had always been a big part of their relationship. Like the best of school friends, their conversations were often about nothing; telling jokes, playing games, sharing dreams for the future. She smiled as she thought of the time a few Christmases ago when they'd trimmed the tree late one evening and played Christmas song trivia. They'd stayed up till almost 2AM, talking, laughing, and simply enjoying each other's company. Those times that had always been a cornerstone of their relationship were now fading quickly into oblivion.

When there was conversation between them, it was guarded and scrutinized as if each were searching for some hidden meaning in every word. All this strange caution generally led to another argument. She really had been trying to repair things. But each time she tried to rekindle the old kismet between them, he would just shut her down or take the dog and leave, leaving her alone and frustrated.

And so her mind wandered more frequently in a new direction: to Jeff Holcomb, the office stud, the good-looking lothario who'd made it clear that if she was interested, he was there for her. She was working on a case with him and had to admit it felt nice to be the recipient of his charm and warmth. She found herself thinking now and then how nice it would be to be with someone who clearly wanted to be with her, and it didn't hurt that he was young and supposedly terrific in bed, or so she had heard.

She wasn't stupid; she knew what Jeff was. But perhaps, just perhaps, he was interested in her because she was different than the young and easily influenced pieces of ass he was used to. Maybe his interest was actually in her, because she was a little more mature, a little bit more of a woman of substance. Maybe.

He'd asked her to go over the case they were working today on over lunch. She'd accepted and found herself looking forward to the meeting, even fantasizing about how their time together might unfold. Looking at herself in the mirror in the bathroom that morning, she had to admit she'd gone to a little extra effort on her appearance. And clearly it worked.

As soon as she arrived at the office, Jeff greeted her with a big smile and a rubbing touch along her bicep and shoulder. She'd smiled back and said, "We still on for lunch?"

"Absolutely, I've been looking forward to it!"

"Good, me too."

She sat down at her desk and started to work. At about 11AM she reviewed the file she and Jeff would be talking about over lunch. She didn't want to be unprepared even though she knew at some level that their lunch wasn't really about the case. At a few minutes before noon, Jeff appeared by her desk, asking in a seductive voice, "You ready for this?"

She looked up at his smiling face and said, "Yes, I think I am." She smiled back and realized she had given him her most wanton face. She got up and they walked together to his car. When they arrived she said, "Should I follow you in my car?"

"Oh no, I'll bring you back when we finish." He flashed a most flirtatious smile.

"OK then."

Next thing she knew he was opening the passenger side of the car. She slid easily into the seat. He drove them to the La Cheminee restaurant, a rather exclusive and expensive establishment that catered to lovers. They were shown to their table and Jeff ordered a bottle of wine, without looking at the wine list. The ensuing small talk soon led to him asking her how her life was going. She found herself revealing information about her troubles with Doug. After about thirty minutes she looked at him and asked whether they should talk about the case.

His gaze was level. "We both have to admit, this wasn't about the case; this was about you and me, knowing one another. I hate the thought of a woman like you having to endure the problems you are. If I was ever fortunate enough to have someone like you, those problems would be nonexistent."

Her heartbeat fluttered in her throat. "That's nice to hear," she stammered, then steadied. "I appreciate it. It means a lot to me to hear someone say it."

"Well you deserve to hear it, and I always will be ready to talk, to help however I can. Listen, I bought you a little gift for all the help you have brought to this case. But I left it in my apartment. How about we swing by there so I can get it for you? Maybe we could even have a drink before I take you back to your car?"

"You didn't have to get me anything." She paused for what felt like an eternity. "But yes, that sounds fine," she tried to say as flatly as she could manage.

Jeff smiled at her, gesturing to the waiter for the check. As she watched him pay and interact with the waitress, she felt a warmth and excitement that had been absent a long time. He made a point to pull out her chair when it was time to go, and escorted her by the elbow to his car. He opened her door and she slid once again into the seat. After he strode around the car and got into the driver's seat, he immediately leaned over and kissed her on the lips with a soft but passionate kiss.

When he withdrew his lips he whispered, "You deserve better, Alisha." She flushed, her body reclining naturally into the warmth of the leather seat.

As he guided the sedan quietly toward his apartment, he laid his hand on her leg just below the hem of her skirt, murmuring to her under his breath and glancing his fingers up and down her bare leg. Before long he was sensuously moving his touch up her leg and under her skirt. She felt a tingling familiar from better times with Doug, and sighed.

Laying her head back, her chest rose and fell in a deepening rhythm. Soon, the outside of his palm was nudging against her panties. She relaxed into the urge that was increasingly overtaking her, until suddenly the image of Doug putting the star atop the Christmas tree singing 'Snoopy's Christmas' jumped into her head.

"No, stop! Please stop." She sat up straight and brushed his hand away. "I'm sorry, but I can't do this."

Jeff complied at once, but it took his expression a second to catch up to his physical restraint. After a moment, he spoke, still a bit softly. "I'm sorry, I just got carried away. I was so excited about the possibility of being with you that I rushed, and I shouldn't have. Please forgive me. When we get to my apartment I will give you the gift and we can just talk. Please, don't let my stupid mistake ruin this for us."

Alisha felt her back further straighten. "Just take me to my car. I'm very sorry."

"No, listen, can't we just talk? Come to the apartment and..."

"Jeff, no. Please, don't make me cause a scene. Neither of us wants that, but I will if you don't take me back to my car, right now."

His face registered defeat. He uttered a clipped "Okay," turned a corner a bit abruptly and headed back to the garage where her car was parked. He said nothing more, sullenly glaring out the windshield and never once turned his glance in her direction. When he pulled up behind Alisha's car, she wiped away tears and said, "Listen, Jeff, I just..."

"Whatever!" His hands flew off the steering wheel in a sign of exasperation but he continued staring out the windshield, avoiding eye contact completely. Alisha instantly knew she had made the right decision. Had she gone through with it, she would have been just another piece of ass in his book, it was abundantly clear.

"Whatever, indeed!" She slammed the door as she left and watched him speed off.

Confused and embarrassed, she sat a while crying in her car, thinking about Doug and what to do. Should she tell him? Maybe that would jerk him into reality and he would then think about their relationship and sit down and talk to her. But what if he instead became enraged to the point of leaving? Her mind raced around the various wonderful and dreadful possibilities for a while longer before she finally dried her eyes, fiercely, one last time and determined to keep the events of today to herself, at least for now. But she was also determined to insist that Doug sit down and talk with her honestly. Their marriage deserved it.

CHAPTER 18

As Alisha had been readying for work that day, Doug left first for work. It had been yet another morning where no words were spoken between them. He was angry, frustrated and quite frankly very confused. He loved her, but things had gotten to a point that being around her always ended up in a fight or with her accusing him of being so caught up in his own world that he was shutting her out. That was crap and she knew it. If anyone was shutting the other out, it was her.

As was typical, though, it was never her fault, always his, he fumed. As he pulled out of the driveway (a little faster than he should), he came to the glaring conclusion that he wasn't happy anymore. And by god, this was on her, not him! Before long, he found his mind wandering to thoughts of Amy McClain. He couldn't deny it; she'd made it pretty clear that if Doug was interested, she would be also. His muscle memory twitched at the thought of the sensuous hand rub. During the few times they'd seen each other since then, she always asked, suggestively he thought, when he was going to let her thank him.

Well, maybe it was time. He picked up his cell phone, pulled over to the side of the road, fished into his wallet for her phone number, and dialed.

"Hello."

"Hi, Amy? This is Doug, Doug Thomas, I'm the one with the dog. I...."

"Oh, Hi Doug, I was hoping you would call sometime. I still owe you, and frankly, I would love to see you again."

"Yeah, well, I was thinking the same thing. Maybe we could get together, you know, get to know one another better."

"I would absolutely love that. By any chance, could you come over today? Maddie is out for an overnight with her grandparents, so we could have some uninterrupted time to talk."

"Uhh...sure, I guess that would work. I can check in with my crew and get them squared for the day and they can cover for me."

"Great, how about 11 this morning. That way I can have lunch ready and before we eat we can have a glass of wine and talk."

"OK, I uhh, guess I'll see you around 11."

"Great, can't wait. See you then."

Doug gawped down at the phone he'd placed in

his lap, thinking, "*that* was quick." Regardless, he was now committed to go. He thought about Alisha and a wave of guilt swept over him, which he violently fended off. *She drove me to this. It will be nice to be with someone who wants to be with me for a change. If she had just tried to work things out, none of this would be happening.* He punched in the number of his assistant on the phone and quickly hammered out the details so Doug could be free for to attend his "lunch" date.

He headed back home at 10:30 to get ready. Salli, surprised by the break in routine, greeted him warmly, but Doug brushed her aside and went to his bedroom to change into a pair of khakis and a nice golf shirt. He brushed his teeth and freshened up at the sink, even putting on a little aftershave as he rehearsed small talk into the mirror. He barely noticed Salli sitting and watching him the whole time. At 10:55 he was ready to head back out. He'd decided to walk to Amy's which meant leaving his car in the garage. Alisha wasn't due home till mid-afternoon, by which time he should be back; if she beat him home, he'd just tell her he'd been calling on some possible clients in the neighborhood.

He ambled toward the front door, solidifying the deception in his head. Salli sat directly in front of the door, a solemn look on her face, steely eyes fixed on Doug. He stopped in his tracks, saying, "Ok Salli, move it. Out of the way." She didn't budge.

"Come on Sal, out of the way, I gotta get going." No movement.

"Salli, what the hell?!" Move out of my way." When she still didn't obey, he reached down to grab her collar, but she barked viciously and then snapped at his hand.

"Salli! No, bad dog! You do not bite at me!" Still, she faced him, head down, tail up, growling quietly.

Doug could feel his blood pressure rising. He boomed at her in a much louder and commanding voice: "Salli, move out of the way, right now!" Her posture remained threatening, and within a split second, she charged at him, lips curled in a frightening snarl that quickly became a loud ferocious growl.

Doug instinctively backed up until he stumbled over the entry-way chair and fell clumsily into it, unthinkingly throwing his arms up to protect his face. But Salli had stopped. He put his hands down and stared at her, amazed at how much her demeanor had changed. She sat submissively before him, ears lowered, face slackened into a begging and frightened look.

Doug sat puzzled for another moment, as she dropped to her belly and began to whine. It was a prayerful, almost human tone she was emitting, as if desperately trying to talk to him. He leaned forward from his awkward slump in the chair, and she immediately sat up and very gently laid her paw on his knee, never shifting her sad and pleading eyes from Doug's own.

Slack-jawed, he stammered, "You ... you knew where I was going. You knew and wanted to stop me from making a mistake. Didn't you? You *knew*. How the...What kind of...?" He sat in shock for a full minute, thinking about what to do. He had convinced himself that he wanted, even *deserved*, to have a fling because the trouble with he and Alisha was all her fault. But his *dog* had found a way to point out to him what a dumbass he was behaving like. He finally looked back at Salli, whose gaze had not shifted from his face, and said, "OK, you're right! I made a list of reasons why I deserve this. And actually I don't deserve shit."

Suddenly she began to wag her tail and she leapt up excitedly. Doug pulled himself from the chair, wandered into the living room and sat down on the couch in a shaken daze. Salli jumped up next to him and laid her head on his lap. He began to stroke her head and suddenly thought of Alisha and how big a mistake this could have been. After a while he said to his loyal companion, "What do you say we take a walk over to talk with Amy." Salli jumped up with a loud approving bark and headed back to the front door.

When Amy answered her front door, she looked down disappointedly. "Oh. I didn't know you were bringing the dog."

"Amy, I can't do this with you today. I don't know what you had planned, but I know what I had planned. And I can't do it. Not that you're not beautiful and I am sure it would have been an unforgettable day, but I am in love with my wife and no matter what problems we are facing right now, I need to try and work them out with her."

Amy's eyes filled tears. After a beat she said quietly, "I knew it. I knew there was a good reason I was so attracted to you. I'd give anything to have someone feel that way about me. My ex-husband was nothing but a self-centered jerk who didn't give two shits about me or Maddie, and when I met you I instantly knew you were the complete opposite, which is just so rare. I'm sorry, I shouldn't have tempted you. I just..."

Doug kept his distance but spoke warmly. "No, don't do that. Don't place blame. This was a series of coincidences that at other times in life wouldn't have meant anything. Let's just move on. And, by the way, someone like you, couldn't possibly <u>not</u> find the right person to be in your life. Thanks for understanding, Amy, and let's stay in touch. Salli loves Maddie and it would be a shame to not let them play together."

Amy smiled gratefully at Doug and Salli barked gleefully, jumping up to rest her front paws on Amy's stomach, then gave a sloppy, happy, lick to her face. Amy laughed and gave her a few good pats on the head before heading back into her house.

Doug and Salli returned to their rightful home, and snuggled on the couch waiting for Alisha.

CHAPTER 19

When Alisha arrived at home at 2:30 she had composed herself and cleaned her red and puffy eyes. She was surprised to see Doug's car at home and immediately went into a slight panic thinking that maybe somehow he had found out about the lunch with Jeff. She entered the house through the garage and came around the corner to see Doug sitting on the couch with Salli.

"Doug, what are you doing here? Did you run out of work today?"

"No, I had a meeting at 11 this morning and it was much shorter than I had expected. So, rather than go back to work I decided to stay here and see you."

"See *me*?"

"Yea, I think we're way overdue to talk. Lish, I know things have been out of whack this past year or more. I know I've been an asshole a lot of the time and I think that caused us to not be who we used to be. I want to fix that, if we can. Frankly I don't know what happened to get us to here, but whatever it was, it needs to be gone. I love you, and I want us back again. Whadaya say, will you talk with me? Do you agree with me?"

Her reply came gushing out. "I have been waiting and waiting to hear you say that. I love you too and *yes* I want to get us back!"

They hugged like the old days and for the next three hours they talked. Many things were said, but none were devastating to their relationship. Both realized there was enough blame to go around, and once the issues were out on the table, they worked on solutions. They agreed that this should have been done much earlier. Neither story about the other two people and the close calls in their lives was told.

At around 6PM Alisha looked at her watch and said, "Where are the kids?"

"They're spending the night with Allen and Jennifer. I didn't want any interruptions tonight. I didn't know how long this might take and it's important. Tonight it's about us."

They went to dinner at their favorite Italian restaurant. They ate and drank wine, laughed, talked and agreed that the real problem they were having was that they had gotten lazy with each other. Over the final glass of wine they both pledged that life would not overshadow romance ever again.

When they arrived home Alisha took Doug's hand and they moved to the bedroom. He slowly and sensuously unbuttoned her blouse and let it fall to the floor. He embraced her and undressed her completely. As he looked at her, he couldn't help but think about what a jerk he almost had been. She was as beautiful as the day he met her. As he lightly kissed her and stroked her naked body she unbuckled his belt and returned the favor of helping him out of his clothes. Then the two fell into bed and enjoyed the next few hours together. Salli quietly stayed on the floor at the end of the bed, wagging her tail, obviously pleased with the outcome.

CHAPTER 20

Dr. William Clark phoned Doug the following Monday at 8 AM sharp. Doug was already at work and answered after just 2 rings.

"Doug, this is Dr. Clark. I hope your weekend was fun and eventful."

Doug thought of his weekend with Alisha, smiled and said, "My weekend was wonderful, on both of those counts."

"Great, glad to hear it. My reason for this early call is that I was truly astonished and impressed by your dog when I put her through some testing. So impressed, in fact, I told the entire story to a colleague of mine in the Chicago area. He also has a great interest in the perception qualities of dogs. Doug, he would like to meet the dog and perhaps do some further testing; at no charge by the way."

Doug sat for a minute and thought. One of the subjects that had come up with Alisha and him was Salli. Both had agreed that Salli had some specials talents, but Alisha had actually felt that

Doug's time with her had become more important and interesting to Doug than Alisha was. She'd been quick to point out that she also loved Salli, but she felt somewhat replaced by the dog.

Although he'd never felt that Salli was more important than Alisha, Doug had to acknowledge the fact that Salli had become an obsession with him. Their joint conclusion to the dilemma had been to assure each other that Salli would be *their* dog. They both would be in on the life of the dog. Except of course, Doug was still in charge of the entire cleanup that goes with having a large dog. As he thought about that portion of the conversation, he smiled.

"Doug? You still there Doug?"

"Yes, I was just thinking about a conversation my wife and I had this weekend." As casually as he could, he told Dr. Clark about the conversation. "I just don't think that this would be the right time to have a lot of fuss over Salli, but I will discuss it with her tonight and call you in the morning. Will that be acceptable?"

"I understand completely," replied Dr. Clark. "I will call my colleague and explain the situation. Perhaps he may have an idea on how to proceed. He seemed most interested about pursuing this. So I look forward to your call tomorrow. Thank you and goodbye. Have a nice day and evening."

After the call Doug sat and thought about the situation for a while. Then he called Alisha and explained what Dr. Clark had proposed. They discussed it for a few minutes and both decided that they didn't want their family pet to be put through a battery of tests, or poked and prodded to the point of missing what was most important; which was enjoying her life with family.

Doug called Dr. Clark the next morning and explained the situation. He thanked him for the time and the interest in Salli but declined for the reasons he explained.

"Doug, I understand as does Dr. Smythe. However, I encourage you and Alisha to entertain this proposal a bit further. Dr. Smythe would very much like to meet you and your dog. He is willing to meet you in Portland next week. To help entice you he has offered to put you and your wife up in a hotel, with the dog of course. And he will fly to Portland to meet with you and all that he asked is one afternoon at Willoughby Park. No poking or prodding, no wires or instruments; just a few hours of observation and interaction. All, at his expense."

"Really? Wow, he must really be interested...and rich."

Dr. Clark laughed and said, "Let's just say he has a very lucrative practice. Doug, he seems fascinated by this and if you and Alisha can swing it for a night or two, I think this would be a good little vacation for you two and the dog shouldn't mind at all. You would be staying at the Imperial Princess downtown close to where Willoughby Park is located."

"Holy crap! He must have a killer practice if he can afford that just so he can meet a dog!"

"Welcome to Dr. Alex Smythe's world. He is a man who generally gets what he goes after."

"Well, I will have to talk to Alisha, but I hope she'll say yes. If you do not hear from me by noon today just assume it is a go."

"Excellent! Once all is confirmed I will send you all the information and arrangements."

Doug immediately called Alisha and explained the situation. As he had figured, she agreed quickly. The Imperial Princess was a very exclusive, elegant hotel in downtown Portland. The thought of having an evening like that together gave both of them the feeling of being special and they agreed that feeling like royalty for a night, wouldn't be a bad thing.

CHAPTER 21

Dr. Clark called and gave Doug all the particulars for the trip. Dr. Smythe would arrive in Portland on Wednesday, September 18. He would take a cab from the airport and meet them at the hotel at approximately noon. They wouldn't be able to check in until 3 PM, so that would be the time they would go to the park and do the evaluation of Salli. Then both parties would spend the night and check out the next day.

Doug then called Dr. Smythe and offered to pick him up at the airport and for him to join him and Alisha at dinner the night of their stay. Dr. Smythe agreed to the airport pickup but declined the dinner invite. He chuckled at Doug and told him that, after a long flight and an afternoon in the park with the dog, he would need his rest.

Dr. Smythe had made all the arrangement at the hotel, including the stay of an 85lb pit bull dog. The management of the hotel was reluctant but agreed when a rather large extra dog fee was agreed to and applied to the bill. With that, the excursion was set. Doug and Alisha were thrilled to be the recipients of such an expensive and exquisite junket.

CHAPTER 22

Ray Allan sat in an easy chair in Melissa's living room, slowly sipping a glass of scotch as he contemplated how his plan was coming together. He'd been with Melissa for nearly two boring years. It was high time to accelerate things. He didn't like to stay with a mark more than a few years anyway, because the more time that passed, the greater the chance something would be found out and the whole scheme ruined.

And frankly he was tired of the whole routine and pretending to enjoy the life of the dutiful "boyfriend" who loved his "girlfriend" and her "sweet little boy." Sex with Melissa had been great at first, but now it was the same old same old. His occasional trip to Las Vegas, where unbeknownst to Melissa he would party with his sleaze-bag buddies and pick up girls, certainly helped. On one trip he'd had a close brush with violence after a man in a bar took exception to a comment Ray had made. The guy had pushed Ray and told him that if he didn't shut up he'd kick the shit out of him. Ray had calmly walked away from the situation to avoid trouble, but after the man stormed out, one of Ray's buddies followed, casing him until the perfect time and place presented itself to bash him in the back of the head and deposit him in the trunk of his car. He then dropped off the quarry for Ray in a desolate part of the desert, where Ray tortured and killed the man and buried him, never to be found again. Sex that night with his whore of choice was very satisfying, even if it was a little rough for her.

Savoring the scotch and smirking at the memory, Ray plotted his next moves with Melissa. So far he had paid out very little to live with her, but the investment fund he'd set up for her had accumulated only about twenty thousand dollars from Melissa and fifteen thousand from sister-in-law Mary. Not great for an almost two-year time commitment, but he was confident all that was about to change.

He'd shown both ladies documentation suggesting substantial increases on their investments, and set up a fake web site where they could keep track of where their money was being invested. He'd cautioned them not to share a lot of the information with others, claiming the fund was one he and his partners saved for only the most select clientele.

The truth, of course, was that it was all a sham he didn't want anyone to look at too closely, especially Clarkie old boy, who knew his way around financial doings. Doug was another source of some concern, even though Ray didn't think he was smart enough to uncover the truth alone. But with a little help there's a chance he could uncover the scheme.

It was time to start pushing a bit harder to get more funds into the account, and liberate Ray from this stupid little town and all these stupid-ass people. That meant getting a little more aggressive with Melissa. So far he had been all sweetness and light. It was time to initiate his standard "final act."

So, first on the list: Get rid of Clarkie old boy. It shouldn't be too hard to arrange for his untimely and untraceable demise, considering how oblivious the bigshot's overconfidence and cockiness rendered him to the ways of the real world.

Second on the list: Be the supportive family member who helps Julianne through her grief by helping her with poor Clark's affairs after the horrible accident. There was always amble opportunity to bilk a grieving widow.

Third on his list: Ratchet up the silky smooth pressure on Mary and Melissa. Especially Mary, with her extra retirement funds. And he'd have to get Melissa to talk up his investment expertise with her family and friends so more of them would get in on the investment too.

Fourth on his list: Take care of that fucking dog, which seemed to have a sixth sense about Ray.

Ray downed the rest of the expensive scotch Melissa's money had purchased for him, and emitted a satisfied "ahhh" of anticipation.

CHAPTER 23

Doug and Alisha waited outside the TSA ropes holding a sign that said 'Dr. Smythe'. Salli waited in the car in short term parking. When Dr. Smythe came down the aisle and saw the sign he waved and called out, "Doug."

"Dr. Smythe, it is a pleasure to meet you."

"Likewise. But please call me Alex. Dr. is so formal, feels like I should be listening to your heart."

"Then Alex it is. I would like to introduce you to my wife Alisha."

"It is a great please to meet you, Alisha."

Alicia smiled and said, "You also, Dr. Smythe."

"No No...Alex, please."

"OK, Alex."

They small-talked about his flight, their drive to the airport, and various other things until they arrived at the short term parking garage. Doug then explained that Salli was in the car and said the doctor could sit up front with him, as Alisha had offered to sit in the backseat with the dog.

"Oh no, absolutely not. My purpose here is to meet the dog. What better way of introduction than to sit by her in the car."

This proved agreeable all around and when they arrived at the car, Salli was excited. Dr. Smythe had heard that Salli was a large intimidating dog, but until he had seen her with his own eyes, he had not realized the entire impact. Doug immediately noticed that Alex had taken a step back.

"She looks like a big old mean dog, doesn't she?"

"She certainly does. I had no idea just how intimidating she is. I had never even seen a picture, only a description from Dr. Clark."

Doug smiled and said, "Salli, come out for an introduction." Salli jumped down onto the pavement and looked at Doug. Doug said, "Salli, sit and shake hands with Dr. Smythe." She obediently turned toward Dr. Smythe; sat down and offered her right paw. Dr. Smythe squatted onto his haunches and took the extended paw.

"It is my pleasure to meet you, Salli." And with that Salli leaned toward the squatting man and laid her head against his chest.

"Seems she likes you and trusts you, Alex. Those are the two big qualities she looks for." He smiled and everyone climbed into the car.

The drive to the park took a little over a half an hour and by the time they arrived and parked, Salli and Dr. Alex Smythe had bonded as friends. Doug and Alisha took a long walk in the park while the next few hours saw Alex and Salli going through a series of tests and exercises that were designed to evaluate the dog's perception. Alex came away realizing that she had extraordinary capabilities. He was particularly amazed that she accomplished the tasks without the enticement of treats. She seemed very pleased to comply with no rewards.

Alex was also very impressed by her ability to appropriately interact with other people and animals. She seemingly knew how to approach based on the initial reactions she got from the other. All in all, he was very impressed by her abilities and thought to himself that she was the best he had ever seen.

Still, he was not inclined to put a category of "special" alongside her name. He certainly didn't detect the ability to read minds that Dr. Clark had alluded to. But he was glad he got to spend time with a certainly remarkable dog. He made a mental note to put her on file and to check in every few months for progress reports. He also wanted to be sure to write an article about her for his next research publication.

As the pair walked back to the car afterward, Doug and Alisha joined them and the trio chatted about the park. When Doug unlocked the car doors, Salli jumped into the back along with Alex. As Doug and Alisha got into the front and prepared to start the trek to the hotel, Salli suddenly barked rather loudly. She then leaned down to where the doctor's feet were and pulled up his leather briefcase. She neatly rested it against his side and then again barked loudly.

Alex looked at her quizzically and said, "You want me to open this?" Salli barked again, wagging her tail. Alex opened the briefcase and found himself smiling in total amazement. There in his briefcase was the wrapped gift he had specially ordered for Alisha to remember her day in the park.

He had, a week before, gone to the Willoughby park website and ordered a commemorative bracelet with her name and the date on it. It had arrived just in time for him to wrap it and put it in his briefcase so he could give it to her before leaving the park, but he had forgotten about it. As he pulled the package from his briefcase he looked at Salli and her expression made it seem obvious it was the reason she had retrieved the case.

He stared at the dog gob smacked until he realized that Doug and Alisha were staring at him.

He then quickly handed the package to Alisha and said, "I almost forgot! This is for you, to thank you for taking the time to put up with me for the day." She said that it wasn't necessary, as she opened it, and then gushed over the bracelet and thanked him profusely. Alex heard very little of it as he just stared at the dog that was enjoying the moment by vigorously wagging her tail.

"Alex? Everything ok?" asked Doug.

"Yes, yes, everything is fine," the doctor said out loud. Then in an almost inaudible whisper he leaned in and said to Salli, "How did you know?" He then remembered that he had thought about the gift as they drove and made a mental note to remember to give it to Alisha before they left the park. "Did you...?"

Salli licked him on the face.

CHAPTER 24

With Salli leashed and muzzled, the three of them walked into the Imperial Princess hotel. It was check-in time, a few minutes past 3 o'clock, and the area was bustling with people. Alisha wandered into the lobby area and was admiring the artwork, content to let Doug and Alex handle the check-in. Salli remained on her best behavior. When they took their place in the line that was waiting to check in, Doug said, "Salli... Attention." She quickly heeled to his left side about a half a foot behind him. From that position she moved at his pace, her eyes fixed on the path Doug haltingly had her on. When Doug's turn to check in came, Salli immediately sat behind him, never moving her body or eyes.

Despite her impeccable manners, whenever passersby saw Salli, they inevitably shifted position and became slightly guarded. Spying the dog, one lady standing by the group at the desk immediately jerked away. Then the whispers started: *"I don't know why those dogs are allowed here!"* *"What are these people thinking?"* *"That creature shouldn't be allowed...it's clearly danger-*

ous!"

Then, as Doug had been predicting in his mind, someone complained to the concierge. Dr. Smythe immediately said, "I'll handle this," went to the front desk and explained to the clerk that the dog had been cleared by management prior to check-in. When the clerk replied dubiously, he responded without faltering: "I want to see the manager, immediately."

After a few minutes Dr. Smythe was explaining to the manager quite matter-of-factly that he had paid an additional exorbitant fee for the dog under the understanding that the dog was his research subject and was under his care and supervision. Also he did not appreciate his guests, the dog, and himself being treated like a criminal element. The manger quickly apologized and said there was no problem and the staff would from this point on be absolutely cooperative.

Dr. Smythe thanked him perfunctorily, then turned toward the other guests in the lobby (most of whose eyes were openly or furtively fixed in their direction). He loudly exclaimed, "My dear friends, I shall ask this only once. Until this incredibility sweet, intelligent, and caring animal makes a single questionable move toward you, I would ask that you not treat her as a menace. For none of you know a thing about this dog and I will assure all of you that she would be a better friend to you than 90% of the human friends you now have." He stood for a moment, tamping down the crowd's anxiety with his confidence, then turned back and stood next to Doug.

Doug looked at Dr. Smythe and said, "Wow, you can be a real hard-ass."

Alex smiled. "I can't say I really blame these people. If I had seen her unknowing in a hotel lobby I may have had the same reaction. However, I have learned over the years that if you try to explain, it goes on deaf ears. If you, however, loudly clarify their bad behavior, the reaction is more conducive to your goals."

"Well I appreciate your concern, but it is something that we deal with. It's precisely the reason I've trained her to go into full attention mode when we are in public. Otherwise she'd want to greet everyone in the lobby, and that wouldn't go over very well. It's too bad, she loves people and would relish the chance to meet everyone."

An older woman standing next to Doug suddenly looked at him and said, "You know you are absolutely correct. I hadn't thought of it that way."

"Well, I appreciate that, but I never blame people for their reactions. With animals, you just don't know their history, so being cautious is not a bad thing. Would you like to meet her?"

"Well, yes, I think I would."

Doug looked at Salli and said, "Salli, relax." She immediately relaxed her stance and looked up at Doug. "Salli, would you like to meet a new friend?" She began wagging her tail and just by looking at her posture anyone could tell she was happy.

"Her name is Sally?"

"Yes, spelled with an i."

"Well nice to meet you Salli. With an i." And Salli lifted her paw up and the lady accepted the paw and shook. The dog's tail began to wag at a more vigorous pace.

At that same moment a man dressed in a baker's apron exited the lobby elevator, holding the hand of a little girl with a rag doll. Upon spying Salli, the little girl, who appeared to be around 3 years old, let loose and ran to the dog. The man had a typical reaction of instant panic, but it subsided quickly when he saw Salli lay her head against the little girl's chest as she hugged and patted her on the head.

The woman who had just shook with Salli looked at Doug and said, "Well she's nothing but a sweetheart!"

Doug smiled and said, "Yes she is. And right now she is in heaven. Meeting new people and having a child hug her, that's what she lives for."

The others in the lobby relaxed and more smiles popped up among the crowd. The man in the apron smiled down as the little girl continued to hug Salli's neck. He gently pulled her away from the hold she had on the dog. When the child finally released her grip, Salli walked gently toward the man, sat down and extended her paw. The man was pleased to accept and shake. He looked at Doug and introduced himself. "My name is Gino. Gino Vincini, I own the bakery across the street. Some of the pasteries in the hotel are prepared by me." His accent was obviously Italian. "This is my daughter Marisa. I want to thank you for allowing her to hug your dog. We lost our dog of fifteen years recently, and she has been sad since that day. This is the first time she has shown this much affection for another dog."

Doug smiled and said, "It was a pleasure. Our dog Salli loves children and right now is having the time of her life playing with your daughter." They both looked at Marisa, who was now cross-legged on the floor with Salli, playing with the rag doll.

"Would it be dangerous if you removed the 'mussel'? I truly hate to see dogs with those on."

Doug smiled and said he was sure it would be fine and removed the mussel.

As Doug did so, the man continued enthusiastically. "If you have some time, I would very much like you to visit us at the bakery. It is right across the street, and it is called Angelo's Bakery. My grandfather started the bakery 80 years ago and it has been with the family since. My father ran the bakery till just 3 years ago and now it is my turn."

Alisha then came to Doug's side and introductions were made. Everyone agreed that they would meet later around 4:30 at the bakery for a tour and some samples. Doug heartily agreed to the meeting, announcing proudly that he was a known fresh bread and pastry junkie. He then introduced Dr. Smythe and he was quickly invited to come over also. "And please, bring your dog," the baker added. "My daughter will be very disappointed if she is not there."

After they were all checked in, Alex took Doug to one side and said, "I would like to talk with you for a few moments before we go to the bakery. Perhaps in the fireside room, around 4? It won't take long but I want to discuss Salli and some of my thoughts about the time I have spent with her." Doug agreed and said he would meet him at the fireplace at 4PM.

*****

At 4:00 sharp Doug and Dr. Smythe met at the hotel lounge fireplace. There was no one else seated nearby so the timing was perfect. They sat down and began to sip from the glasses of wine that Alex had ordered from the bar.

"Doug, you have an amazing animal on your hands. She is far and away the most intelligent and perceptive dog I have ever seen. Much more so than most humans I know and have treated. In fact I will go so far as to say she has perception abilities that are extra-sensory." He let the pause sink in as Doug gawped at him, then continued. "Most humans could not have done what she did today. All the tests and exercises we did, she flew through those with no effort at all. But that's somehow the least of it. The most startling thing she did all day was *after* the tests. He then proceeded to tell the story of the forgotten gift for Alisha that Salli had "reminded" him of. "Doug, I have no idea how she knew, but I am 100% convinced she did know. That is amazing and quite frankly a little spooky."

Doug looked at the doctor with a quizzical look and paused. After a moment he leaned in conspiratorially to Dr. Smythe and told the broad strokes of the story of his "almost" extra-marital affair. Dr. Smythe's face slackened into an astonished and unbelieving look. It was his turn to pause. His eyes gazed out into the distance, darting back and forth in perturbed thought. Eventually he spoke again, with great animation. "Holy shit, Doug. What kind of an animal is this? I have to say that she seems to have the ability to read minds. But that can't be, I have studied minds of human and animals my whole life and I cannot say that I ever gave that a single thought, except to say that it was pure poppycock!"

Doug's gaze remained steady and humble on the doctor's eyes. "Alex, I still am a ways from saying she can read minds." He took a beat, as if shy to continue his thought, then proceeded in a hush. "I do believe she is able to sense things...all kinds of things, things that no one should be able to sense, but she does." He stopped again, probing the doctor's expression for signs of ridicule, but happily found none. Then with a tone of what could be taken for pride he continued his confession: "It's hard to explain but she seems able to *connect with* people she knows."

The doctor was piqued with scientific curiosity. "I would like to study her further. I may be able to get some specialists that could help, since this is a phenomenal animal and it would be an absolute shame to not investigate her talents further."

"Hmm, I... I don't know...," Doug stammered in reply. "She is a special dog, but I don't want her life to be ruined by an endless battery of tests. Poked and probed for the rest of her life. She deserves better than that."

Dr. Smythe looked a bit surprised. "Doug, I wouldn't let that happen. That is not what my practice is about. I would respect your wishes as a family."

"I know you mean that, doc, but I also know you can't *promise* that. Others involved wouldn't have that same compassion or compunction." He waited a beat, his gaze steady. "You know it in *your* heart too."

Alex sighed and stroked his chin for a minute. "Yes…you're probably correct. It could end up as an endless onslaught of questions and pressure from others to see the dog and test her for this and for that."

Doug's eyes softened in relief. "After all, she's our dog, and she loves us as a family. I couldn't do that to my family, let alone to her."

The doctor sighed again, this time in acceptance. "I get that, I hear you completely. But let's stay in touch. I'd love to learn more about Salli and her accomplishments. Who knows, perhaps as she gets older we can look at other research possibilities." Doug smiled as Alex continued. "In the meantime, I would be very appreciative if you could at least let me take some blood tests and at some point allow me to do some imaging of her body and brain. Perhaps we could schedule a trip to Chicago for you and perhaps your whole family." The doctor smiled back warmly at Doug.

"That we can do. Thank you for understanding."

Right then Alisha and Salli appeared at the entry to the fireplace lounge. Alisha chatted with Alex for a few minutes after greeting him, again inviting him to join them for dinner. Again he refused, saying he was tired and had to travel the next day. He winked at Doug and encouraged them to go and have a great and perhaps romantic dinner. Then the four of them headed across the street to Angelo's Bakery.

CHAPTER 25

When they arrived they were all greeted by the family, with Gino kissing Alisha on each cheek. He introduced his wife Maria and again his young daughter Marisa. The first thing he did was to pour glasses of wine for everyone and invite everyone to sit at one of the three customer tables in the front of the store. The bakery had a small courtyard that the front windows overlooked where three more small tables sat. His shop had closed at 4PM to the public and this was time that he had to visit with family and friends. Gino spoke proudly of his ancestors and especially his grandfather and father who had ran the bakery before he took over.

After a while he brought out a loaf of baguette bread that Doug swore up and down was the best he had ever tasted. Gino laughed and was extremely pleased. They talked and laughed for about 30 minutes and all that time their daughter Marisa and Salli played in a separate area behind the counter of the bakery. Doug could tell that Maria was nervous about her small child being alone with an 85lb Pit Bull. She would occasionally get up to check on the two, as did Doug. Each time she found Marisa smiling and Salli constantly wagging her tail while gently playing with Marisa. At one point Maria found her little girl sitting on the floor "reading" a book to Salli, whose head lay in the child's lap as she looked contentedly at the pictures. The mother couldn't help but motion for everyone to come and take a look and share in the sweetness of a newfound friendship.

Gino then invited the group to tour his bakery, an idea everyone heartily agreed to. First up was the kitchen, where he briefly explained what all the different equipment was for as he walked them through his early-morning daily routine to produce a wide array of tasty bread and pastry treats. He was particularly proud of the new ovens his father and he had put in a few years earlier, noting proudly how the slate-surfaced gas ovens had improved the quality and taste of his products.

He then took everyone up to the second floor to tour the family's living quarters. Through the front door the first view was of the living room and just to the left a well-appointed kitchen with all new gas appliances. The living area was impeccably decorated with a touch of old Italy intertwined. There were two bedrooms: a master suite with a separate bath and gas fireplace, and a smaller room opposite the living room that was beautifully decorated for Marisa. A separate bathroom was next to the child's room. When the adults peeked into the little girl's room, they once again found her playing happily with Salli, this time under the crib.

After everyone's murmurs of appreciation and comments on various interior design choices, Gino took everyone back out the front door and up to the third floor, to the office where he and Maria managed the business. Among various pieces of stored equipment and a store of neatly organized cleaning supplies, Gino made a point of showing off his newest purchase: two large outdoor propane heaters for use on chilly afternoons to encourage customers to lounge outdoors in the fresh air.

The man was obviously very proud of his bakery, his home and his family, Doug was thinking as he, Alisha, Salli, and Alex left the bakery, leaving behind their sincere gratitude to Gino and Maria for the food and wine and hospitality they'd shown them. Doug promised to stop by the next day to buy more bread and pastries for their return trip home. The group walked back across the street engrossed in conversation about how fun the visit had been and what a great family they were. Alex also remarked about how Salli was an absolute darling with the pint-sized Marisa.

Upon their arrival back at the hotel, Doug tried once more to encourage Alex to join them for dinner. But once more Alex demurred. "I want you to enjoy tonight as a couple. Now go on and get out of here and enjoy. I'll see you tomorrow in the lobby around 11AM and we can enjoy a cup of coffee before I leave for the airport." They shook hands with a mutual smile and said goodnight.

CHAPTER 26

Doug and Alisha left Salli safely resting in the room to enjoy their 7:45 dinner reservations at a very nice and well known restaurant called *La Vallauris Portlandia*. They ordered wine and told the waiter they'd enjoy it for a bit before deciding what to eat. Doug looked at Alisha across the candlelit table, reaching out to take her hand. "You look as beautiful as the day I married you."

She blushed, smiled and said, "You know that was 22 years ago?"

"I do remember. In fact you may be even more beautiful than before."

"You big flirt! But keep it up, I enjoy hearing you say it."

"It's true you know, I think you are the most beautiful woman in this restaurant, and probably all of Portland."

She smiled at him seductively and took a slow sip of the Beaujolais. After about half an hour they ordered their dinner, and then followed the delicious French cuisine with a marvelous desert of Tarte Tatin. They left the restaurant feeling full and extremely happy, and decided to stroll for a while before returning to the hotel. They wandered around a lovely park and through a few quaint streets, twice stopping for a nightcap.

By the time they ambled back into the hotel lobby, it was closing in on midnight. Doug surprised Alisha by asking the clerk to extend their stay another night if they could arrange the same room. After handing over a $20 tip and his credit card to secure the arrangements, Doug pulled Alisha close and whispered behind her ear, "I didn't want this to end quite yet." She squeezed his hand and kissed him in return. They rode the elevator to their room, opened the door, said their hellos to Salli and took her out for a final chance to relief herself for the night. They then fell passionately into the bed while Salli curled up happily on the floor beside the loving couple.

Doug awoke at 6AM and hurried to take a pee. When he tried to sneak quietly back into bed, Alisha murmured, "that's a really good idea" and stumbled into the bathroom to do the same. Once back beneath the cozy hotel bedding, she rolled over to face Doug and said, "Know what else would be a really good idea?" They made love again, and then slept till nearly 11AM. When they awoke they realized they'd agreed to meet Alex at 11 for coffee. Doug quickly got himself looking presentable and hustled down to meet Alex, who was already there.

As Doug hurried over to the table, Alex smiled up at him and said, "Have fun last night?"

Doug smiled and said, "As a matter of fact…"

"Good, I like you two together. Listen, before Alisha comes down, let me mention something. I spoke to some colleagues this morning and we all agreed that we'd like to keep tabs on Salli and maybe someday meet again. Think that would be possible? We of course would respect your wishes around the conditions for the arrangement."

"Yes, of course, I will be happy to keep in touch. I just don't want to make her a prodigy that we never get to see. We want our dog to be just that: our dog."

"Understood."

About then Alisha and Salli showed up and all of them sat and had coffee and Danish pastries for breakfast. Then talked and laughed and, when it was time for Alex to leave, shared hugs and good wishes all around. Seeing Alex off in his Uber to the airport, Doug and Alisha set off to continue their walking exploration of the general Portland scene, this time with Salli at their side. They stopped by Angelo's Bakery for a late lunch and chatted some more with Gino and Maria. Salli and Marisa played on the sidewalk and then a bit up in Marisa's room. When it came time to leave, Marisa grabbed Salli by the neck and kissed her on the head. Salli responded with a kiss to her face, eliciting laughter all around.

Back at the hotel, the threesome relaxed in the fireside room and talked and reminisced about Alex and the Vincini family. When they headed back up to their room around 6PM, Salli jumped up on the bed and proceeded to get a good nap in. Marisa had definitely tired her out. Doug and Alisha dressed casually and went down to the hotel bar. They sat at a table and had a few drinks, then ordered a small plate of appetizers for dinner. Around 8PM a local band started playing and they stayed, listened and danced till almost 11PM. Knowing they had to check out the next day they called it a night and went back to the room. Both said they were too tired to make love again, laughed, and tumbled into the bed, locked in each other's arms.

After Doug and Alisha had overcome their exhaustion thoroughly and pleasurably enough to settle sweetly into sleep, little Marisa across the street awoke with a start.

She sniffed the air at an unknown odor, her face in an instinctive scowl. Her head jerked toward her closed bedroom door when she heard a sound in the kitchen. Eyes wide, she dashed back under the covers, scrunched her eyes tightly shut and started to quietly whimper in fear.

Across the street, Salli's head rose quickly in the dark hotel room. She began whimpering simultaneously with Marisa.

CHAPTER 27

Doug and Alisha were awakened by Salli's loud and insistent barking. Glancing at the clock, Doug immediately shushed her, knowing that their hotel room neighbors would not appreciate a 2AM wakeup call. Salli ignored his command, instead barking louder as she ran to the door to the hallway. Doug stumbled out of bed and angrily jerked her back by the collar, snapping, "Goddamn it Salli, shut up!"

Alisha suddenly sat up straight. "Doug, something must be wrong. You know she only does that when there's a reason."

Doug shook his head to drain some of the sleep from it, his eyes widening as he darted a look between Alisha and Salli and then back again. Gasping, "You're right!" he released his grip on the dog's collar and said to her, "What is it, girl? What's wrong?"

Salli kept her attention on the door, directing her rhythmic alert barks in that specific direction. Understanding, Doug opened the door. Watching the powerful Pit Bull bolt unaccompanied into the hallway, Doug threw on a pair of pants, grabbed some shoes and ran after her. She was already at the elevator, urgently barking back at him, when Doug rounded the corner. He hit the down button about 20 times, his muttered "C'mon c'mon c'mon" drowned out by Salli's barking, and when the elevator doors finally opened they both flew in so fast they almost bounced off the back wall of the enclosed space.

Doug slapped the lobby button with the heel of his palm. Salli stood with her snout only inches away from the doors, her insistent bark replaced by a fixed stare. When the doors opened again, she exploded from the elevator car like a rocket. She crossed the lobby in a flash and ran headfirst into the wheelchair entrance button on the main doors. A trick she had learned earlier in the day. That positioned her to speed through the narrow door opening at precisely the moment it was wide enough to accommodate her.

By the time a sprinting Doug also made his way outside, Salli was already almost fully across the street to the bakery front doors. As he ran, Doug's eye caught on something unusual: a light was shining in the bakery kitchen area of the otherwise dark building. He did a confused double-take mid-stride when he realized the light was flickering. Just then the flickering light expanded and the whole front of the bakery building exploded in fire. Doug tumbled back into a somersault, arms instinctively raised to protect his head from the fall and his face from the fireball surging out from the front windows, hurling shattered glass all the way across the wide street to the hotel entrance.

Gaping up in shock from the pavement through splayed fingers on trembling hands, Doug saw Salli sail through a broken window, leap over a falling banister and fly up the smoke-filled staircase toward Gino, Maria and Marisa's home. Doug jumped up and after Salli, all adrenaline, but a new explosion of glass and flames, accompanied by the terrifying rumble of crumbling masonry, repelled him. For a seemingly endless moment he stood swaying, legs and arms akimbo, in the street as though he were impersonating a deranged basketball player who doesn't know which way to pivot. His eyes were darting again, but soon enough they landed on the hotel entrance, and his feet followed their lead. He sped back to the hotel entrance just as quickly as he'd just sprung from it, propelled by his predominant mental image: that of a terrified and worried Alisha upstairs, but she had already made it to the lobby.

By now the bakery building fire alarms had gone off and people torn violently from their rest at the hotel were calling 911. The sound of fire engines grew in the distance, but the fire took no notice. Fueled by gas from the baking ovens, another explosion ripped through the ceiling of the first floor, eagerly consuming the residence kitchen and living room, and licking its fiery path toward the stairway connecting the second floor back to the safety of the street.

After the first explosion Gino and Maria had darted from bed, tearing open the door to the living room only to expose a massive flame-spitting hole in the floor before them and a hellish glimpse of what was left of the area, now just an inferno of fire and toxic smoke.

"Marisa!" Gino bellowed across the hallway, hands splayed on the doorframe as he physically restrained himself from sprinting out toward certain death. He could vaguely feel his wife's arms wrapped round him and her body convulsing in choking cries behind him, and distinctly heard his heart pounding behind his eyes as his brain scrambled to identify a manageable path to his daughter. Finally he heard her from behind her closed bedroom door—her hysterical wailing was even louder than the roar of the flames threatening to engulf them all. The flames were even starting to lap at his daughter's bedroom door.

Horribly, Gino knew he couldn't reach Marisa without melting his own flesh and then hers once he tried to escape with her. Helpless to conceive how he could cover the infuriatingly short distance across the flames and collapsed floor to rescue her, he shouted at her to stay put, that Daddy was coming to save her, despite having no idea how or if he could. Maria's convulsive crying turned to a machine-gun assault of screaming blows across his back. "Do something! Why don't you do something?" she screeched in her own helpless terror. He wrenched an arm behind his back to try to comfort his wife, continuing to call out to Marisa to stay put, wheels in his brain spinning frantically.

Salli had reached the second floor just before the second explosion. Its force blew her into a wall where flames quickly surrounded her. The blast had also destroyed the passage from the second floor to the ground floor. Without delay she leapt up the stairs a bit further toward the third floor, then turned back and fixed a concentrated gaze on a small strip of splintered flooring that hadn't yet burned leading to the doorway to Marisa's room.

Crouching low and building momentum with a quick shimmy of her hips, Salli launched herself down from the stairs through the flames, landing with a tenuous sway of gravity on the narrow, weight-see-sawing shard of hardwood that hadn't yet contributed to the inferno outside the girl's room. Flames snapped up at Salli through the gaping hole in the floor, and were taking hold where an ember had struck the little girl's door about halfway up. As soon as she landed Salli turned to Gino, whose shouts of comfort to Marisa had turned to exclamations of total astonishment. "Salli, is that you? How did you get here!?" Salli barked acknowledgement in Gino's direction, turning back to survey the center of the door as the flames did their work there.

Helpless to deny the building horror of his wife's wails or the undeniably rising heat within the painted wood frame, Gino could not fathom how the dog he'd met the day before had suddenly landed out of nowhere on the other side of the fiery abyss that separated his wife and him from their child. His body had flung back from the doorframe in surprise, but Maria's hold on his torso remained as strong as her cries of torment. Time stopped for a moment as Gino's nerve endings registered all unfolding before him. His hands were cupping the sides of his face as if in concentration. Milliseconds later he shot a fierce look at Salli, pleading in a commanding voice, "Please! Save my daughter!" Salli stared at him for an instant, head tilted, before turning back from the flames dancing at her paws to assess the fire climbing up the closed barrier of Marisa's door.

Standing sideways on the smoldering hardwood plank among the encroaching flames, Salli suddenly sprung through the burning center of the door. Marisa stood screeching in her crib, but fell silent as soon as she saw the dog, even thrusting her arms out with the adorable clawing reaching "come here" gesture of a toddler.

Salli leapt across the hot and smoke-filled room and into the crib. Marissa wrapped her arms around the dog in the fierce embrace of a familiar. Salli shook the child loose, seemingly callous, but all the while with her nose and mouth carefully pushing the little girl down to the mattress to lay her face-down.

Next, with an artful jaw grab onto Marisa's diaper and nightshirt, Salli placed her paws up on the top railing of the crib and jumped out of the crib with Marisa securely held in her jaw, holding her head high to protect the child from a hard landing on the floor. Carrying the child in this way, Salli raced back through the doorway, but the flames had risen further, preventing even a view across the hallway to where Gino stood watching her and cheering her on.

The determined dog turned to the side to protect the baby from the flames while surveying the territory with a peripheral glance. There! The opening to the stairs was still visible. In a split second and with no hesitation she jumped, using the remaining hardwood plank as a catapult to send the pair flying through the flames and back onto the stairs leading to the third floor.

It was a hard landing, and Marisa burst into fresh tears. Salli released the child and started licking her to calm her down. The distraught girl once again reached out for the dog, and Salli allowed her to wrap her arms around her neck. Salli then began slowly ascending to the third floor, with Marisa's diaper touching down at each step, her hands clamped around Salli's strong neck, her wet face nuzzled in Salli's big flat chest.

Gino had continued cheering on this amazing sequence of events from his post at the burning doorway. Just then, a firefighter emerged through the exterior window of Gino and Maria's bedroom, flanked by a small crew. Gino tried to explain what was transpiring on the stairs but the firefighters kept interrupting him, insisting that getting him and Maria to safety first would speed the rescue of their daughter. Gino and Maria hastened to follow their directions, hoping to get the focus back on Marisa as soon as possible. The remaining fire crew quickly realized that the hall outside the bedroom was impassable and followed the couple down the fire escape.

Looking up at the inferno from below now, Gino and Maria were grasping each other, mutually inconsolable as they watched the fire spread.

Just then the fireplace in the master bedroom room erupted in a geyser of fire. A gas main had erupted in the room.

Meanwhile Salli and Marisa had reached the 3rd floor entry door from the stairs. Closed. Salli had deposited Marisa on the threshold and was trying to turn the doorknob with her teeth, but it wasn't working. She'd resorted to barking down the stairs for help when the little girl, softly sobbing, stood up, looked at the dog, stopped crying, and reached up with both hands to open the door. She then looked at the dog for approval, giving her neck a fresh hug. After a few seconds, Salli gripped the girl again in her mouth and dragged her cautiously across the smoke-filled room toward the window, keeping a watchful eye out for signs that the fire had breached the space. Sure enough, the geyser of flames had burned through the floor from the second floor and was headed toward the propane heaters stored in the room.

Salli wasted no time but moved with careful deliberation. She put down the child, burst through the glass of the closed window to create an opening, jumped back into the room, picked up Marisa carefully and maneuvered the bundle and herself gingerly out the broken window to the fire escape. Because of her caution, the broken shards had left only a few cuts and scrapes on the pair, who were now ascending the fire escape toward the roof, the baby rocking almost comfortingly as she bumped against the dog's chest with each step.

A fireman on the second-floor fire escape on that side of the building looked up and saw what was happening. He shouted in amazement, spurring a handful of his nearby colleagues to raise their helmeted heads to the astounding sight of a dog carrying a young girl up the fire escape.

The group of firefighters rushed up the escape, racing fearlessly past flames now spewing from almost every window that prevented Salli from going toward the firemen. But when one of the propane tanks suddenly erupted, an entire section of wall was blown away above them, and the firefighters had no choice but to retreat to the street, leaving the vulnerable baby in the jaws of a strange dog at the top of the fire escape.

Almost immediately afterward the second propane tank erupted and the roof of the building began to visibly collapse. Salli kept methodically climbing.

By now a large crowd from the hotel and surrounding neighborhood had gathered on the street below to ogle at the wonders and horrors unfolding above. But they were not on the street with a view of the fire escape where Salli was bravely protecting Marissa at least for the moment from certain death. Doug and Alisha were among the group gathered on the street, watching in disbelief as the building readied to collapse in front of their eyes, their beloved dog and a young child trapped amid the chaos.

Nearby, Gino and Maria kept trying to explain to the fire crew what they'd seen the dog do upstairs, but in all the commotion no one was listening or thought to tell them where their little girl was now, out of sight of her parents. Doug and Alisha spotted them and rushed over to try their best to console them. All Gino could say, repeatedly, was, "Your dog, your dog!"

Then someone from the crowd gathered further down the street yelled, "Look! That dog has the little girl on the fire escape." Doug whipped his head around and quickly ran to where he could see. Before he knew it Gino was at his side yelling, "See! She is saving my Marisa! I saw her through the fire and begged her to save my little girl. She is fulfilling the promise she made to me!"

Gob smacked, Doug embraced Gino and reflexively pointed up, one arm embracing a fellow father as the two men watched Salli continue to climb up the increasingly unstable metal fire escape toward the near-collapsing roof with Marisa still safely in her jaw's grasp.

Doug was annoyed to notice a man standing close by filming the whole thing on his phone.

What kind of sicko derives enjoyment from tragedy was the though flashing through his over maxed mind. But this blind judgment was interrupted by another big blast, this one knocking the fire escape off its brackets, leaving the towering tunnel of metal swaying widely in midair.

A loud collective gasp went through the crowd like a shot. Every soul watched as Salli re-secured her hold on Marisa, placed her front paws on the ladder rungs to the roof and incrementally pulled herself and the little girl up the last few rungs until they'd safely reached the top and stepped onto the burning roof. Flames shot straight up in the air all around them. Screams and wails rising from the street below were inaudible above the roar of fire. Everything looked hopeless.

Yet Salli stood calmly, carefully situated on the two-foot-wide brick foundation that surrounded the collapsing roof of the building. She quickly assessed the situation and looked to the building standing next to the burning structure. That building was only two floors high, a small apartment building. But there was a deck attached to one of the back apartments on the second floor, about 12 feet down from where the pair was perched and about 10 feet across the alley some 35 feet below. Without hesitation and still holding baby Marisa in her mouth, Salli took off at a full run. Marisa swung back and forth as they picked up speed.

As the dog leapt into the air and toward the deck below, the crowd below screamed. Some covered their eyes while others gawped at the incredible scene they were witnessing. Salli tucked down her head to clear the roof of the deck, twisted her body to hold Marissa away from the point of impact, and landed hard in a chaise lounge—sending it skating across the deck and into the wall. The aluminum arm of the chaise snapped as it hit the wall, driving a sharp metal shard into Salli's chest.

She let out a yelp of pain, then lay still as the air no longer went easily into her lungs. Marisa was screaming and crying. Within seconds the firemen were on the scene. Hurling open the sliding glass door to the deck, they stopped in their tracks. A dog lay half on and half off the chaise lounge, with an arm of the chair impaled into her side. The crying girl had her arms around the dog's neck.

CHAPTER 28

Two firefighters immediately began checking the little girl for any serious injuries that could prevent them from transporting her to the waiting ambulance. They laid her down and checked her movements and determined there was nothing serious. By then a group of medical responders had gotten to the area and began to secure her to a gurney to take her down. She was quickly taken to the ground floor where her frantic parents met her and were told that it did not appear she'd sustained serious injuries but needed to be taken to hospital to be sure. Gino and Maria rushed into the ambulance as the doors started to close, but Gino stopped them and said to one of the firefighters, "The dog! Please save the dog! She saved my daughter's life." Alisha and Doug, flanking the ambulance doors and fully focused on Gino's daughter's safety, spun around with the reminder that their seemingly magical dog had saved the day but now lie in mortal distress.

Unbeknownst to them all, one of the firefighters had indeed stayed with Salli. After she knew the little girl was being properly attended to, she returned to the side of the dog. Salli's respiration was very shallow and she could tell each breath caused pain. She radioed to her chief at the scene and asked what to do about the dog that was in peril. "Sir, she needs immediate help!" Can we transport her to DoveLewis Emergency?"

The chief, who knew well what she'd done to protect the child, replied: "You're damn right we can! I'm sending two medics to help stabilize her and then we will deliver her in my truck."

Next thing, the two medics came sprinting up the stair with Doug and Alisha at their heels. The medics did everything they could to stabilize her and contain the bleeding. They left the aluminum shard in her side and transported her down to the ground floor and into the chief's truck. Everyone piled in and with sirens and lights blaring the truck took off to the veterinary emergency center. The crowd gathered on the street began clapping and cheering with spontaneous cries of, "Way to go dog!" "Get well Hero!" "God be with you!" "We love you!"

Once at DoveLewis, Salli was taken immediately into an emergency room. A vet quickly looked her over and ordered x-rays. She was given a shot for pain before being wheeled off for the procedure. After a few short minutes the vet came in and showed the x-rays to Doug and

Alisha. The fire chief was still in the room and said to the other firefighter, "Time for us to get back, Sally."

Alisha turned and looked at the firefighter and said, "You're a Sally too?"

The human Sally smiled back and said with a smile, "Yes. As a matter of fact, I think that's why your dog's such a good firefighter, I figure it has to be in the name. Chief, with your permission I would like to stay."

The chief looked at Alisha and Doug and both smiled and nodded their approval.

"Absolutely, and firefighter Sally, may I say, you did a helluva job today. Well done! And when you see the dog, tell her she is now my newest hero." He turned to Doug and said, "When it's time you can get a cab or an Uber to wherever you need to go. It's on the city of Portland." He handed Doug a card with a validation code on it.

Doug thanked him and shook his hand. He then turned to the vet for the report.

The vet explained the injury and told them that Salli needed surgery right now to remove the aluminum shard and to repair the wound. He received their permission and had them sign the necessary papers.

"Can we see her first?" Alisha asked.

"Of course, follow me."

They went to a room where two assistants were preparing her for surgery. Alisha noticed that firefighter Sally wasn't present. She quickly went back to fetch her, then all three wished the doggo well, told her they were proud of her and, all gave her three simultaneous kisses. Salli responded by trying to lick them, but the exhaustion and the drugs had started to take over. Before long her prone canine body was ready to be wheeled into the surgical room.

The stay for Doug and Alisha in the waiting room was tortuous, with worries of Salli and Marisa and Gino and Maria and so much else whirling in their hearts. Time moved torturously. They tried to chat lightly among themselves, but to no avail. Minutes turned to hours. Finally, as the sun peeked through the waiting room windows, the vet appeared. His smile relieved a lot of angst immediately, and then he spoke.

"She is alive and responding well. That's one helluva tough dog, I gotta say! She's not out of the woods yet, but I am very positive. She is stable. Blood pressure is good and her heartbeat is strong. Of course she is on some pretty heavy duty antibiotics."

"Can we see her?" Doug asked.

"Yes, of course, but the drugs are making her

sleep. That is the best medicine right now."

"Thanks, doctor," Doug and Alisha said tearfully, shaking his hand. Firefighter Sally, still nearby, patted Alisha's arm and winked as she went by. This gave Alisha the chance to make sure human Sally could accompany them to the recovery room.

Once there, all three gathered around valiant Salli. They stroked her lightly and spoke to her in soft and reassuring tones. In response, Salli opened her eyes and began wagging her tail. Everyone including the vet and the assistants all smiled and gave encouraging words. When the vet said, "We better let her sleep," Alisha looked at Doug and said, "Doug, get Sally home and then get some rest and take care of the kids. I want to stay with her."

She laid a hand on Salli. Doug smiled and said to the vet, "Take care of my girls."

The vet winked and said, "You know we will."

Sally put her hand on Alisha's shoulder, and Alisha rose up and hugged her. "Please stay in touch."

"Count on it."

Doug kissed Alisha, then Salli and left to take kind human Sally home after a long shocking day for everyone.

Alisha stayed with Salli at DoveLewis for the next three days as she recovered; and she did recover.

CHAPTER 29

Salli's release day had grown into an anticipated media frenzy. The phone videos taken the night of the fire had dominated the local and statewide news. More than that, the bigger media outlets had gotten hold of the footage and made the story a national phenomenon. All the national TV affiliates were hailing Salli as a hero. Lester Holt had exclaimed on his evening news program: "In a world that needs heroes right now; we have one that will simply amaze you" followed by a slow motion clip of Salli and Marisa sailing through the air to the safety of the adjacent building. Lester ended with, "An amazing rescue by an amazing hero. And best of all, everyone is alright."

Now, leaving the emergency vet clinic, Doug and Alisha were stunned by the hoards, in the hundreds, of well-wishers and media. When they opened the door a loud cheer went up that actually made Salli take a confused step back. She quickly recovered when seeing little Marisa as the first person to greet her at the exit. The child immediately went to Salli and wrapped her arms around her neck and hugged. Salli responded with huge tail wags and so many kisses it was impossible to count. Of course every moment was caught on camera by the throngs.

Gino and Maria were among them at the forefront of course, both crying as they also hugged Salli and repeatedly told her and the media that the dog was a hero. Doug and Alisha gently pushed their way through the crowd of reporters answering questions and thanking the vets that saved Salli's life. Once back in their car, finally ready to head back home, Doug said, "Holy shit! I wasn't expecting that!"

"Right?! Did you ever think we'd be media sensations?"

"Hell no! But to be fair, we're just the eye candy, big girl back there is the star." He shot an admiring glance in the rearview.

Alisha laughed, doing the same. "You're sure right about that!"

Doug was silent for a few minutes, his stare now pointed forward, out the windshield.

Alisha asked lightly, "What's going through your head right now?"

Doug sighed and slightly shook his head in a serious manner.

After a moment he said, "What do we have, Lish? I mean, how the hell did she know about that fire? When I got down to the lobby that bakery showed no signs of a fire, and the night clerk had no idea, but she knew. How? Maybe we do have a dog that possesses special abilities? I mean, look at the things she's done."

Alisha glanced back at the sleeping Salli, quiet for a moment with her thoughts. "I don't know... What I do know is that she's definitely different than any dog, or person, I have ever met. She does seem to know things that shouldn't be known to anyone. The Candice and Kathleen event, that night, still amazes me, not to mention the rest of the family."

"When you stop and think about it now, do you think maybe it's worth talking with Dr. Smythe some more?"

"Oh Doug, I still worry about that! She's the family dog. And I don't just mean *our* family. All of the family loves her. If she became a research project, she wouldn't be happy and sure as hell the rest of the family wouldn't be happy."

"Yea, I get that. But what if she is something truly special? What if she has something akin to extra sensory abilities?"

"Well, what then!? Send her away for experimentation? Put her through a battery of tests and studies and whatever else they think of? Look forward to performing an autopsy to find out what her brain holds versus other dogs? Not to mention that every nut job in the world would be coming to us asking her to predict the next lottery ticket or where their long lost uncle is. No. I don't like it, Doug, and I know you wouldn't either, once you saw what it really meant."

"Wow, you went right to the dark side," Doug laughed in reply. "But I get it, I do. She loves this family and it would be wrong to deprive her of a normal existence, not to mention how it would affect us."

The two sat silent most of the trip home.

CHAPTER 30

Ray Allan positioned himself in front of the sliding glass door that overlooked the apartment building's courtyard. He looked at the time and saw that it was a little before 4:00PM. Melissa would be home around 4:15. She always arrived home around that time when she worked the day shift; she said she liked getting home as quickly as she could to be with him for the whole evening. *Stupid bitch...*he thought, *like I give a shit.* The real Ray Allan was starting to surface more and more and he knew it was time to move forward rapidly. Tonight would be the start to the final push. He had decided that he would maneuver quickly and efficiently to gather more money in the fund and then finally disappear. He was sick of this asshole family and he wanted out.

Tonight he would show a new side of himself to Melissa. The brooding, insecure and down-trodden sweetheart whose feelings were hurt that he couldn't even get the love of his life to help him succeed. He gulped his scotch and poured another healthy pour into his glass. He sat down and waited for her arrival. The scotch had successfully calmed his raw nerves, which was necessary for the upcoming charade.

It was 4:18 when he heard the front door open; he smiled at the thought of her consistency. "Hi sweetie, I'm home." He purposely did not answer. "Ray? Sweetie? Where are you?" She rounded the corner from the hallway and saw him sitting in the chair overlooking the courtyard. "Hey, didn't you hear me calling you? Ray?" She looked at him slumping in the chair and sipping his scotch as he solemnly looked out the glass door. "Ray, is something wrong?" He simply shook his head. "Honey, what is it? Talk to me, did something happen?"

"I'm a lousy failure." He looked up at her with a pained look on his face. "I had a meeting today with my partners in Las Vegas, and we're not making it. There's just not enough money coming in to support us. And look at me, living here with you and not even able to carry my weight."

"Oh baby, that's not true."

"Yes, it is. I'm not carrying my fair share and I know it. Your family is going to hate me and you by association before long."

"Oh Ray, that's not possible." She moved toward him but he stood up and went to the glass door and leaned against the wall.

She tried again. "Honey, you do so much around here and you do contribute. You make money, I know you do. And not to mention how much your investment of my money has paid off. I gave you $15,000 less than two years ago and today it's worth almost $24,000. That's serious money. And, what about Mary's investment? Her $10,000 is now worth $15,000. Ray, don't you know I love you and so does Jamey?"

"But even after proving I can make money for you and Mary and others, still your family stays away from me. Let's face it Meliss, they don't trust me and never will. Look what I've done for Mary and even she won't invest another red cent. And as for the rest, hell they barely even talk to me. I've tried Meliss, I want to be part of this family, but it's just not happening."

"Ray, it will happen. Maybe this is my fault. I should've got you more involved with the family, I could've talked to them more about you and shown them what you can do. I promise I'll do that now and I'm sure you'll get more interest from the family. Because you're wrong, you know? They do like you, I'm sure of it, and I'm sure they'll do more investing with you. Especially when I show them the returns you have gotten for me and Mary."

It was time to turn on the humility. "Oh Meliss, I didn't mean to make you feel like this was your fault. It's just that I'm really worried about my future and I don't want anything to screw up what I have with you. It will be great to have you help me with your family. I want to be part of it all. I want to be family, and I know I can do it, especially with your help. I love you Meliss." He took a hesitant step back toward her.

It was the first time he'd said those words to her. She rushed forward in a sob and melted into his arms in a passionate embrace. Ray wrapped his arms around her and hugged her tightly, resting his chin on the top of her head. Out of her view, his eyes half opened and his mouth curled into a malevolent grin. He thought, *"Perfect. I become vulnerable, and she rushes in to save me by falling on the sword. Works every time."*

CHAPTER 31

After a long and persuasive conversation with Alisha and a promise to not allow Salli to become a media darling, Doug and Alisha accepted an invitation to appear on the local evening variety show "The Portland Scene." It aired right after the 6:30 news and featured in-depth interviews about a variety of interesting events, but mostly focused on the fun and positive happenings in and around Portland. The host for the show was a young and energetic woman named Michelle Waverly who was quick to point out that her friends called her Micki, and that everyone watching could call her that because, "You're all my friends."

As Salli entered the stage, the small but vocal studio audience all stood and applauded, letting loose with whoops and hollers. Salli relished every moment. Doug and Alisha hadn't realized what a ham she could be. She excitedly jumped toward the audience in a circle motion and barked all the while, wagging her tail vigorously. The audience loved her immediately and encouraged her to continue. After a few minutes they got Salli to the chairs where the guests sat, where Micki was waiting to give Salli a hearty series of pets and pats. She was a bit surprised and taken back when Salli slopped a big kiss on her, right in the face. The audience went crazy with laughter and applause.

Micki questioned Doug and Alisha about the fire incident, stoking the crowd's sympathies even more by playing all the videos and asking to hear all the details about how the rescue played out that night. Afterward, she surprised Doug and Alisha by bringing out the Vincini family. Gino, Maria and Marisa gushed over the dog and told their version of the story and how they were sure Salli was a special gift from heaven sent to save their daughter. The only awkward moment came when Micki asked how the dog knew about the fire that night, since their hotel room did not face the street. Doug and Alisha just looked at each other and finally Alisha said, "We really don't know, it's kind of a mystery to us also. We can only guess that she has the ability to sense danger, especially with people she has made a connection too, which she had with this wonderful family."

Micki didn't miss the opportunity to heighten the drama: "You mean a sort of ... sixth sense?"

Alisha paused before saying, "We don't want to go that far, but she seems acutely in tune with people she knows."

Micki pushed on. "But…if she is able to predict things like this, couldn't it be said that she has a special ability?"

"Well, yes, but, …" She glanced at Doug with a *help me* look.

Doug jumped in. "We certainly don't think she has 'special abilities.' This is not a commonplace incident. I mean, it's not like she's predicting the stock market or the next earthquake. But I, we, do feel that all dogs have a perception ability that is much greater than they are ever given credit for." He looked into the eyes of Micki with a look that said, *let this go*.

She picked up on the look and said, "Well, Salli, whatever you have, we certainly were glad you had it that night. Ladies and gentleman when we come back we will find out about the extraordinary story of how Salli came to be part of the Thomas family."

*****

Ray Allen sat on the couch with Melissa and Jamey, smiling and laughing along with them at the interview with Doug and Alisha. But what was really going through his mind was dramatically different. *"Yea, real cute. That fucking dog is gunna make life difficult for me. I know the goddamn thing doesn't like me and if she starts letting that be known to the rest of the family that could screw up my plan."*

The plan was shaping up nicely. Ray had orchestrated an intimate talk with Melissa after his performance the other night. He had been emotional and adamant that he didn't want her talking to her whole family, claiming he didn't want to come across as a pity project. He had masterfully manipulated the conversation to ensure Melissa would indeed gently persuade Alisha's siblings to talk with him. The idea was that Mary should further invest with him to make even more money, and Jennifer should invest in a college fund. When Melissa had offered to talk to Clark and Julianne, he had cautiously said no, he would do that himself in due time, saying he had a special investment designed specifically for couples like them. Then the subject of Doug and Alisha came up and Ray was very quick to say he was not comfortable with talking to them because he was convinced that Doug did not like or trust him. He was careful to humbly suggest it was probably a sort of "big brother" syndrome and that he understood, but he would want to be very careful in approaching them. Perhaps, he suggested, Melissa could instead simply work on Doug to accept and embrace Ray as part of the family. Melissa had agreed to the whole concept and Ray was quick to thank her and express again how much he loved her. He'd even been able to call up a few crocodile tears as he said that she was an amazing woman and how lucky he was to have found her.

Now, as the "The Portland Scene" episode neared its finale, he smiled a smarmy grin of cocky arrogance at the TV, thinking, *"A couple more months of this asshole family and I should have enough to bail out after a job well done."* He fixed his eyes on the dog smiling happily on screen, seated proudly between Doug and Alisha as Micki finished up the show. *"Unfortunately,"* he thought darkly, *"you can't be part of it, you ugly fucking pot hound."*

At that very second the elated dog suddenly closed her mouth and whipped her head directly toward camera, staring into living rooms across town with cold steel eyes. Slowly the dog's hackles on the back of her neck rose. Ray Allan jerked up, lost his conniving grin and suddenly felt the hair on the back of his neck rise also, as if someone had just walked over his grave.

CHAPTER 32

As Clark readied for work that morning, his mind was on the presentation he was to make to the Alvarez Mexican Cuisine restaurant chain, now the largest Hispanic food chain in Oregon. He kissed Julianne goodbye and she smiled and wished him *Good Luck*. If Clark was successful in the presentation he would sign a lucrative account to his employer, The Oregon Bank. He was confident; this was what he had become known for, convincing high profile accounts to abandon their huge conglomerate national companies for a local and more attentive smaller company. He had already practiced his closing line many times, but he did it again as he drove to work; "At the Oregon Bank, you're not one of many small ducks in a large pond; you're the big duck in a small puddle." He smiled as he said it; it had become his signature line.

When he pulled into the parking structure next to The Oregon Bank corporate offices, he waited as the guard rail electronically read his transponder and then lifted, allowing him entrance to his private parking space on the second level.

He was proud of the private parking space as he was with many other attainments he had received over the past few years. His hard work and dedication had paid off. After 20 years of work with the company, he had finally achieved the success he wanted for himself and his family. He thought of Julianne, how he had met her nearly 25 years ago and they were married a year after.

They had set a goal to live a life that allowed financial freedom and the ability to travel. Children had never been in the mix and that was OK for both of them; they concentrated on their shared dual life, and Clark had been able to provide the life they both wanted. Parked now, he gathered his briefcase, opened it to check on the presentation packet and other papers, closed it and opened the car door. As he shut the door and pressed the lock button on his key fob, he peripherally caught a glance of a figure moving toward him dressed completely in black. He also saw the shining of the 8" blade mere seconds before it was plunged into his left side just below the rib cage and then forcefully driven upward till it punctured his heart. He inhaled a deep breath and as he fell backward onto the cement floor of the garage, air slowly escaping his lungs.

He lived just long enough to feel and see the murderous stranger empty his pockets and wallets of money and pull off his watch. As the stranger stood up, he smiled through his mask and said, "Thanks Buddy." Then the man roughly dragged Clark to the front of his car and left him on the ground out of sight of the garage camera.

The assailant then quickly moved to the exit and was down the two flights of stairs to the street in a matter of seconds, careful to avoid any cameras. He had taken off the black sweater, the black ski mask, the black gloves, the latex gloves, and the latex head cover, stuffing all into his pants. He was on the street again in a matter of seconds, very careful to stay out of view of the street light cameras. He celebrated by popping in to a bagel and coffee shop to enjoy a leisurely bite, and then caught the Max train out of the area.

Meanwhile, the life drained out of Clark's body and his head lolled to the left. His final view was of the underside of his car.

CHAPTER 33

Ray Allan was quietly proud of how meticulously he'd orchestrated Clark's death, down to every small detail. He had followed him, learned his routine, and checked out all the details of his parking structure, especially the cameras. He knew exactly where Clark went every morning and how he got there. The key to an unnoticed murder was always the timing.

Through his legwork, Ray knew the parking structure had an attendant at the guard station Clark always used. The main duty of that guard was to smile and wave at the monthly members, to take money from those who were not members, and to answer questions and give directions to those who did not know the rules of the building. The guard had an assistant who would carry out those same duties when he was otherwise occupied. The nearby camera monitors were watched by someone about 90% of the time, according to Ray's careful observation. The other 10% of the time the attendants were distracted taking care of customers. Based on Ray's cagey reconnaissance, there were no other places where the monitors were viewed.

That meant a man wielding a knife could enter the building using the back stairwell, easily avoiding sight from cameras. It meant another man could cause a slight commotion at the entrance to pull both guards away from the monitors, leaving the knife man open to take care of Clark, rob him, and drag him out of sight, and exit to the street without notice.

The "commotion man" would have ample time to flee the scene before being spied on camera too. Ray nodded at his own cleverness. Both were from out of town and had taken circuitous routes to ensure they couldn't be identified. By the time the police played back the tape, it would be too late to find either of the men and it would go down as one of many unsolved robberies. Genius.

CHAPTER 34

The doorbell pealed, and Julianne hopped up. She opened the door to the unwelcome view of a very solemn police officer. As she stood looking at the officer, her throat tightened and her mouth became dry. Her stomach knotted up and she felt she may vomit at any second.

The officer said, "Mrs. Westphal?"

She couldn't speak; she simply nodded and uttered an acknowledgement.

"Are you married to a Clark Westphal, who works at the Oregon Bank?"

The tears started to overflow as she closed her eyes and sobbed, "Yes." She knew what was coming next.

"Mrs. Westphal, I'm sorry to have to inform that your husband Clark was killed this morning. I am very sorry to have to bring this news to you."

Julianne stepped back and immediately fell to the floor of the entryway.

The officer stepped in and knelt beside her, "Mrs. Westphal, allow me to help you. Can you make it to the couch in the living room?"

She simply nodded. The officer could tell at a glance that she'd gone into shock; her face was pale and her eyes stared straight ahead.

"With your permission, I will help you over to it."

Again she nodded.

Once at the couch the officer sat her down and looked into her eyes and said, "Mrs. Westphal, I need to call an ambulance for you. I think you're in shock and require immediate medical attention."

She then looked at the officer, shook her head and said, "Doug, call Doug."

"Doug? Who is Doug?"

"Brother, he'll know what to do. Please."

"Of course, do you have a number for him?"

"My phone, in my purse." She pointed to the counter in the kitchen.

The officer made sure she was securely seated and fetched the purse quickly back to her. "May I have your permission to retrieve the phone?"

Again she nodded.

He handed her the phone and she went to favorites and pushed the line labeled 'Brother Doug.' She put the phone to her ear and looked blankly into the officer's face.

The officer could hear the voice who answered. "Hey Jules! How's it going today?"

She started to speak, "Doug. ... Clark, ...gone..." She closed her eyes and started to cry.

"Julianne! What's going on?"

The officer took the phone from her and immediately said, "Doug, this is Officer Connors of the Portland Police Department. I'm with your sister Mrs. Westphal, and I have delivered some devastating news to her and she needs your help."

"What news?"

"Her husband Clark was killed today."

"Oh shit! Oh shit...Oh my god...how?"

"We can talk about that later. Do you want me to transport Mrs. Westphal to the hospital and you can meet her there?"

"Yes, but where? I live in Salem and it will take me about 45 minutes to get there."

Suddenly Julianne took back the phone and sobbingly said, "Doug, come to the house, I don't want to go to the hospital."

"Jules, it probably will be best for you. They might be able to give you something."

"Like what? Can they give me Clark back?" She started to get louder and Doug sensed she was on the verge of hysteria.

"Okay, Sis, okay. Julianne, listen. You stay right there and I will get to you ASAP. OK? You need to stay quiet till I get there. You understand?"

She nodded and said "Yes."

"Let me talk with the officer again."

She handed the phone over and Officer Connors said, "Yes Sir?"

"Can you stay with her till I arrive?"

"Yes sir, there is also a woman coming over from Human Services to sit with her till you arrive. Actually she is here now. I requested her within a few minutes of informing your sister of the death."

"Great, I'll be there as soon as I can."

"Drive carefully sir, getting here is more important than getting here quickly." He disconnected the call.

*****

Doug yelled to his crew that an emergency had come up and he would be gone the rest of the day. As he jumped into his car he thought immediately of Alisha. He picked up his phone and called her.

"Hi Doug." She sounded cautious.

"Lish, listen. Clark was killed this morning and I am on my way to Portland to be with Julianne."

"Oh god, Doug. How…?"

"Don't know yet but Jules seemed in pretty bad shape. She wanted me there right away. Cops wanted her to go to the hospital, but she said no, not till I got there."

"Oh Christ Doug, I knew something was wrong today."

"What…what do you mean?"

"Salli has been beside herself all day. Whining at the door and looking out the windows and barking. She hasn't sat or laid down all day. I just knew something was wrong."

Doug sat with his whirling thoughts for a few seconds and then said, "We can't think about that now. First priority is Julianne. I will call you when I get there."

"Do you want me to come up and meet you?"

"No, at least not for now. If I need you to come up I'll let you know. I think first I better assess the situation and see if she needs to go the hospital. The cop told me there was a lady from human services there to be with her. I will certainly want to get her advice.

Lish, I hate to do this, but can you call the rest of the family? Don't call my Mom, I will call her later, but call the rest and give them the news, and let em know I'll call later to update them when I know more."

"Of course. I love you Doug."

"Thanks and I love you too. Talk to you soon."

*****

When Doug arrived at her house, Julianne collapsed into his arms, crying uncontrollably. He could do little except to console her and give her love. After a while she started to calm or at least tire out. Doug gave her a tender look and said, "Sis, I'm so sorry. And I'm here, and not going anywhere except to be with you. I want to talk to the Officer. Will you be OK for a few minutes?"

"Yes, go ahead."

Doug gave the human services worker a glance, which she acknowledged and moved next to

Julianne, talking sweetly with her as she held her hands.

Relieved, Doug tracked down the officer and asked the question that had been burning in his brain: "What happened to Clark?"

The officer blankly informed him that Clark was murdered in what appeared to be a common robbery. He explained that the murder had been caught on tape, but that as of the present time there were no suspects or leads. He proceeded to ask Doug some very basic questions about Clark and asked if Doug could be present when he questioned Julianne. Doug agreed, shell-shocked.

Julianne became very emotional again when she heard that the death was a murder, and Doug was glad to be there to console her. After a long and emotional period, the officer again gave his condolences on her loss and his assurance that the police would work hard to find the killer, before summarily leaving the house.

The Human Services representative also left, but not before retrieving some prescription drugs that had been prescribed. She left her condolences and a phone number for Julianne to call if she needed anything.

When it was just Doug and Julianne, she again began to cry and did not stop until she fell asleep on the couch with the help of the prescription sleep aid. Doug quietly began to make the phone calls to the family as promised.

CHAPTER 35

Alisha, informed by Doug, joined in the effort. She made her first call to Melissa, which was appropriate, given Julianne was her sister. Not surprisingly, Melissa became highly emotional. She immediately tried to call Julianne and Doug but, getting no response from either, made a motion toward her car to drive to her sister's house. That was when Ray Allan then took control of the situation. He had rehearsed this many times and was ready for just this situation.

"Meliss? What's wrong, baby?" He moved quickly to her side and wrapped a comforting arm around her.

"It's...Julianne...Clark was killed today."

"What!? Clark, he's dead? Oh my god...how?" In his mind he carefully plotted his questions. One small slip could ruin the whole scheme.

"No one said how, and I didn't ask."

"Of course, it was a stupid question. It was just the first thing I thought of. It doesn't matter how...just that it happened. I'm so sorry baby.

How can I help?" He started to choke up and his voice quivered, "This is devastating, Julianne must be in complete shock!"

"I need to get to her, Ray! Alisha said Doug was on his way to be with her and I've tried to call them both and there is no answer. But I need to be there with her. She's my sister and she needs me!"

Ray registered the expected panic in her voice and calmly said, "Listen to me, baby. Right now you're too upset to drive. And you don't even know where she is. She might be in the hospital or a friend's house, or somewhere else. I think you need to stay put for a little while until we hear from Doug, and we'll keep trying to call him."

She started to cry and Ray wrapped her in his arms tightly and said, "Just let it go baby, just let it go."

And she did. For the next 5 minutes she cried into his chest and sobbed about her poor sister and how great Clark had been and how this was going to devastate Julianne. Ray continued to hold her tight and kiss her head and give supportive comments, all the while ruminating silently on all the ways he would benefit from Clark's death. He smirked as he thought about the turmoil he had caused.

The phone rang a few moments later and Melissa jerked up from Ray's chest and quickly answered, "Doug?"

"Yea, it's me. I'm with Jules now. She's a mess... can you get up here?"

"Yes, are you at her house?"

"Yes, but drive careful. Driving fast won't change anything, so be safe."

"I will. Doug how did this happen? Was he in a car accident?"

Doug hesitated, but decided to tell her the truth as he knew it. "No...he was robbed going into work this morning and the guy killed him."

"Oh my god! You mean he was murdered?!"

"Yes, some son of a bitch stabbed him and killed him, then took his money and everything he had on him."

"Oh Jesus Doug, this is awful. Just plain sick! Poor Julianne, she must be...We'll see you soon, I'm going to have Ray drive me."

Doug didn't say anything, but his silence spoke volumes.

"Doug, he is very upset and just wants to help. And quite frankly I need him right now."

"OK, ok I'm sorry. Of course, it makes sense. I'll see you guys in a little while. Drive safe!"

Turning in tearful desperation, Melissa said, "Ray I need you to drive me to my sister." He nodded and went to get the car. In a daze Melissa grabbed a few things, made arrangements for Jamey at a friend's house, grabbed her purse and went to the car, already running. Ray backed out and headed to Portland.

En route to the freeway he asked, "Meliss? Did you find out something? It sounded like you heard something about his death?"

"He was murdered; by someone who robbed him as he was going to work."

"Murdered?! Dear god. By some asshole thief?!"

Melissa started to cry again and sobbed "Yes, over a small robbery."

"My god."

After that they were silent for about 20 minutes while she sobbed and Ray rubbed her shoulder. Then Ray spoke up, "I want to help. And I can really be of help!" He shot a calculated glance at Melissa.

"What do you mean?"

"Well, I know I'm jumping ahead but I'm thinking about the family consequences here. Clark and I were essentially in the same line of business: finance. I just mean that I've helped other people in the exact same situation before, and I can do it again. I can handle the back side of expenses and finances while the rest of the family helps Julianne out in her greatest time of need." Melissa gave him the helpless and expectant look he anticipated, and he continued with a somber tone.

"I mean, in this dreadful time she is vulnerable to scammers and hidden charges. The last thing she needs is to worry about money. I helped a woman in Las Vegas who had invested in my company and lost her husband in a car accident. I took care of everything and saved her a ton of money and heartache by just watching and making sure everything was taken care of. Making sure the funeral arrangements were followed properly with no hidden charges. Taking care of the life insurance and making sure it was done quickly and properly. And there are additional expenses she will be looking at, and those need to be handled and scrutinized."

Melissa's countenance was wan but appreciative, exactly what he'd calculated. He continued. "Despite the immediate trauma, this is a time when the immediate family will be overloaded with grief and confusion, dealing with police reports and inquiries. I hate to say it, but it's a time when mistakes can be made. Julianne and your family need to be together and help her heal, not worry about the crazy finances involved with a sudden death. But I can help. This is an area I know very well."

"Ok, yeah. That all makes sense...we can talk to Julianne and probably get something set up so that you can handle all that for her." She paused, confused, but to his relief added, "That's so great of you."

He remained measured in his plan. "But not tonight. We'll talk to her in a day or two when she's clearer. And we won't have to worry about talking to Doug; maybe this will be a way for him see that I ain't so bad."

"I think you're right. And I think Julianne will feel the same." She leaned over and put her hand on his leg and her head on his shoulder.

In the darkness of the car, absorbing her trust, his lips curled once again into an arrogant smirk.

CHAPTER 36

When they arrived at Julianne's house, the two sisters fell into each other's arms and cried. Ray quietly walked over to Doug and extended his hand. As they shook Ray said, "Doug, I don't know what to say, other than this is the shittiest thing I have ever heard."

"Melissa told you the circumstances?"

"Yes, and I can hardly believe it. Clark was one of the nicest guys I can imagine. He seemed so gentle and easygoing that it just boggles my mind that some scumbag would target him. I can't imagine what you're going through." He looked at Julianne and Melissa as they held each other, then said in a lower voice: "Listen, I don't want to get in the way. Maybe you should go over with your sisters. They need you. Just know if there is any way I can help, I'll be here."

Doug suddenly felt a bit guilty about the way he'd thought of Ray. "Not at all, you're not in the way. Thank you for bringing Melissa here and taking care of her. It's appreciated. And yes, you probably can help."

Ray nodded to him and then motioned at the girls with eyes saying, *they need you now*. Doug smiled at him and turned and went to his sisters and they all wrapped in an embrace.

*****

The phone calls and well wishes of everyone came pouring in as the rest of the family learned the details of Clark's death. Alisha had now joined Doug and assured Julianne that they'd stay for as long as needed. Their mother stayed a couple of nights too, and even Mary spent one night there to pitch in. Allen and Jennifer stayed at home and watched over their kids along with Robbie, Chloe and Salli. Everyone did their part to help in some way, even Ray Allan.

The fact that his motivation was completely different than everyone else's was known to no one but himself. He remained mister helpful; ensuring that everyone in the family had whatever they needed no matter what it took for him to accomplish it. He doted on their mother and made sure she was comfortable and well cared for. When the others couldn't be there, he spent time alone with her and treated her like the queen mother.

He also spent as much time as he could with Julianne. He was attentive, sweet and unwaveringly understanding. He took care of her whenever he could and with the greatest of tender care.

His patience in waiting for a perfect opportunity paid off one evening while he sat with Julianne after everyone else had turned in for the night. She had talked to him about Clark, sharing stories of the fun times they had together and sobbing through her disbelief that she had to go on without him. Ray had listened and soothed and comforted her, his arm around her shoulder as she cried, expertly hiding his disgust at the snot she was leaving all over his sleeve. She looked up at him and said, "You've been absolutely great."

He kept his most humble expression on his face. "I just want to help you through this. I know by talking with you and getting to know you over the past couple years that you will get through this, but it just rips me apart to see what you have to go through. You've got a great family and I'm just hoping to become part of it." He then traded out the humility pose with his most practiced face of sorrow.

"I know you do Ray, and you will. Melissa told me that you want to help with the financial end of this mess, and that you have actually done this for another person who went through ..." She started to tear up again and Ray patted her hand gently. She breathed deeply, pulled out a Kleenex (a bit too damn late, Ray thought acidly) and continued. "It is true you've had experience with this type of situation?"

A perfect lure! He nodded silently and gave her hand another pat. She sat up and composed herself a bit. "Well," she went on, "I want you to know that I signed papers today to make you a signer on my checking account, and I am so grateful that you have the knowledge to help me on this." He feigned a look of surprise, reeling her further in. She leaned toward him. "Oh don't worry! This of course will be temporary, and I hope it won't be too much of a burden on you. But I'm already getting calls about payments and arrangements that I just don't have the strength or knowledge to deal with. Thank you! Thank you so much, Ray." She exhaled in relief. "I can't tell you what a weight off it'll be to have you to handle all the calls and payments associated with Clark's death. And Melissa told me you want to surprise Doug, which is so selfless and sweet – so I want to assure you I understand that the rest of the family doesn't need to know about this until you think the time is right. You will have to take the forms I signed, and a new signer form with ID, to the bank and give them to Henry, but that is all. I explained to Henry at the bank the situation and we were able to get this taken care of via phone."

Ray filled his eyes with tears, pausing for even greater effect. "This means so much to me, Julianne. Your faith in me to help you through such a miserable time, it's just one of the most special gifts I've ever received."

Her eyes filled again with actual tears, which she tried to laugh off this time. "Just be sure you take good care of me."

Ray laughed back lightly, squeezing a single tear from his eye with a nod and a smile, and one last comforting pat of her hand—the hand that signed his way right to where he wanted to be. Julianne had no reason to suspect his smile reflected a much darker thought: "Stupid simpering cow -- you have no idea how good I'll fix it!"

*****

Ray also doted on Mary the night she stayed. She finally stopped him and ushered him quietly away from the others. "Ray!" she sternly whispered. "People will be suspicious if you keep this up."

"No...they'll be suspicious if I don't. Look, Mary, I know what happened was wrong. But it happened and I feel just terrible about it. Many times I have wanted to confess to Melissa, but haven't had the courage."

"Ray, you can't ever tell her! You promised. Yes, it was a big mistake, by both of us, but it has to be kept a secret! You cannot tell her!"

"I just feel so guilty." He chuckled inwardly at that one, since of course the last thing he felt was guilty. He had given Mary every chance to invest more money with him, but the bitch had kept dragging her feet. Having sensed that Mary felt a bit of an attraction to him, he'd managed to quietly arrange a private meeting at a bar near where Mary lived. After a few too many drinks, one of which had a little additive of Ketamine powder, getting her into bed was easy.

The next morning he'd played the dazed, hungover, guilt-ridden family member disgusted with himself for not having been sober enough to behave properly. It really worked perfect.

Now he was reveling in the role of disgraced boyfriend who couldn't live with himself unless he came clean.

Mary's eyes darted around to be sure no one was in earshot before continuing her whispered plea. "Ray, no! You can't confess to Melissa! That would destroy her and this whole family along with it. Please Ray, don't let our mistake, a mistake that won't ever happen again, ruin everything...please."

He soaked it up, outwardly playing the tortured soul of a good-at-heart man who just can't catch a break. "It's just ... it's just that I've been under so much stress lately. I'm trying to fit into this family and it just isn't working. And my business is faltering right now and I just feel like I have failed Melissa in so many ways. In this one way at least, I want to do the right thing by her."

"Ray, you simply can't tell Melissa. Listen, if your business is down, I can talk to some of my flight attendants friends to see if they would consider investing. I've already been planning to close one of my IRAs to invest with you, so that should help convince some others to do the same. I like you, Ray, and you make Melissa very happy. I don't want that to come to an end because of one stupid mistake that she doesn't need to know about. Hell, I don't even remember that much about it." She sighed deeply and looked at Ray with pleading eyes filled with shame.

Ray gazed at her with the most benevolent look he could muster. "Wow, you really are a special person, Mary. I see now how you're just acting out of the best wishes for your sister-in-law and for me – I hadn't thought of it that way. You're one in a million, really. You're right -- even though I will never forget our night together, I can see that it's best kept between us. The more I get to know you and your whole family, the more each day I realize how lucky I am and how special you all are to me, each in your own way."

She smiled at him in relief and squeezed his hand

in thanks. As she turned to leave his look of kindness melted into a stone cold gaze at her back as he thought to himself, "What a sucker. Always nice to have another dumb cunt in my corner."

CHAPTER 37

Allen and Jennifer planned an evening to take everyone staying at their place to see Julianne, and called to ask if it would be ok to bring Salli along. With Julianne's approval, Doug told Allen to bring her but to plan on taking her back that same night to limit extra stress on the household. The only ones who couldn't be there on the scheduled evening was Jamey, who had an important school activity first thing the next morning that required some preparation and plenty of shut-eye, and Ray, who'd agreed to hang back at his and Melissa's apartment so he could shuttle Jamey to and from school for it. Ray was quite proud of himself for arranging this, knowing the less time he spent around that damn dog, the better.

When Allen and Jennifer arrived, Doug and Alisha warmly greeted them and their children and of course gave their dear Salli much love, overjoyed to be reunited with her. But within a few minutes Salli moved away from them and toward Julianne, laying her head in her lap. Julianne couldn't help but invite her up on the couch next to her, and in an instant Salli had hopped gracefully up and settled into a position that was comforting to Julianne without being obtrusive. As the group chatter continued, Salli remained insistently by Julianne's side; if Julianne shifted position or got up for something, so did Salli. At one point Doug told Salli to leave her alone, but Julianne scolded him and said she was fine having a canine shadow—it made her feel less bad about having not shaved her legs in days. They all laughed at that and rested easy for the rest of the evening. Julianne seemed genuinely restored by having everyone there, exuding a sense that she felt safe, and comforted, and could maybe start believing that everything would be ok in a life without her beloved Clark.

When it came time for Allen, Jennifer and all the kids to leave, Doug chimed in, "That means you too, Salli my dear." But Julianne was having none of it. "Oh Doug, can't she stay? She won't be any trouble and I would so like her to be here." She kneeled down and gave Salli a loving two-handed pet that spread from the top of her head to behind both ears and ended under her chin and into the scruff of her broad chest.

Salli turned her tongue-wagging smile and "Joker" grin from Julianne up to Doug, and Doug melted.

"Aw, well I guess so ... if you're sure, Sis?"

"Yes, I can't quite explain it but I suddenly really want her here."

"Alright, I guess you're off dog duty then, Allen."

Allen looked at Doug and then to Julianne and said, "I think it's great. She was no trouble, but clearly she's got a greater calling here, eh?" Everyone chuckled except Julianne, who couldn't stop giving sweet Salli loving chest scratches.

Goodbyes were said all around, and with Salli tearing herself from Julianne's side to give all the kids happy kisses, the evening came to its happy end. Salli returned to Julianne's side as soon as the others left, and when Doug suggested bedtime for everyone Julianne demurred. "I'd like to just sit here for a while with Salli. It's very comforting to be with her."

Doug smiled, "I get that, Sis. She can feel what you're feeling and has the empathy to make you feel better." He smiled at the two of them sitting on the sofa, "I'll leave our door open a bit, just in case she wants to sleep with us. But I'm betting that unless you say no, you will have a bedmate tonight."

*****

Ray couldn't stop congratulating himself on his cleverness to avoid the scene. When Ray dropped Jamey at school that next morning, he told him he'd be back around 4:30 to fetch him after practice.

As soon as Ray arrived back at the empty apartment he started riffling through all the papers and information he had brought back from Julianne's. He had easily gleaned all the information he knew he needed about the checking account she'd added him to, but had frustratingly failed to get information about her other accounts, which he'd tried to explain were important for him to have visibility into to properly protect Julianne.

But he'd succeeded in getting access to a key one: the life insurance policy that Clark had on himself. He'd told Melissa it was important for him to have that information so he could be sure it was a guaranteed policy and not one that the insurance company could reduce the amount of payout based on the growth of the policy. He assured her that he knew Clark had been savvy enough to get the right policy, but carefully explained that it was crucial for Ray to watch the company and be sure they performed ethically. Julianne had bowed to his supposed expertise in the area and gave him a copy of the policy.

Now, scanning the documents he formulated the next stage of his plan. Around 3:30 that afternoon he called his partner in Las Vegas.

"Hi Jackson, good news. I'm officially a signer on the widow Westphal's checking account."

"Oh shit, that is good news! How much does she have in the account?"

"Not enough. Not yet anyway--there's only about six thousand. But don't worry, I have a plan. So listen up and take down this information." After relaying the account information, he continued. "Now, we've gotta get the death benefit payout into the checking account, and I know that ain't gunna be easy. I'm no fool. I know it may have been easier to kill mister big shot Clark Westphal than it will be to get hands on this money. That's where you come in. I don't know exactly what needs to happen but I'm guessing it will require at least her signature. Probably more. So I want you to call the insurance company as a random inquirer, and find out what it takes to get a life insurance deposit switched to someone's checking account."

"Can do. What's the payout to her?"

"300K."

"Holy shit, man that is one *fuck* of a score if we can pull it off! How long before the insurance company is meant to release the funds?"

"About a week. I checked the policy and learned it has a quick return because there are no restrictions. Old Clarkie Boy didn't want his beloved to wait to enjoy his death. So get busy and find out all the info we need and get back to me by noon tomorrow. I want to act quickly before the wrong family members find out that I'm a signer. I want to execute the plan on this shithole family within a week. The sooner I vanish with money for you and me both, the better. Got it?"

"You bet I do. I'll talk to you tomorrow."

Ray hung up the phone with a triumphant smile. What would definitely be his biggest score was coming together beautifully. He and his partner would probably have to leave the country for a while, but that was ok--a little tropical isle action would be a good for a change of pace. He stood and gave a leisurely stretch to luxuriate in his genius. From the top of his stretch he brought his wrist down and checked his watch. It was time to get ready to pick Jamey up from school. Everything was coming together perfectly. With a sneer he gathered up all the incriminating documents and turned to head to the kitchen, only to find himself looking directly into the wide, fear induced, suspicious eyes of Jamey, who'd somehow materialized in the room. How much had the boy heard or seen?

"Oh hey there, kiddo!" Ray tried to say casually, struggling to subdue the surprise and concern that coursed through his body that made him significantly short of breath.

CHAPTER 38

Meanwhile, Mary and Melissa were having lunch together. Mary was awash in her lingering guilt about the night she'd spent with Ray a few months ago. But that wasn't her purpose for the lunch; she'd managed to sufficiently push that out of her head. Instead, to assuage her conscience, she was keen to let Melissa know that she had arranged to put more money into Ray's financial investment fund.

She explained that, to support Melissa and Ray's relationship, she'd been able to close an IRA of about $25,000.00 from the airline that had been producing less than 5% per year—she was certain, she said, that the funds would get a better return if applied to help with Ray's business. To veil her guilty reasons for the offer she effused about Ray's financial skills, assuring her sister-in-law that she was confident Ray could produce results. Swallowing back the bile in her throat, she reminded herself that if this move helped keep certain secrets, all would be for the better.

As their small talk meandered across the family

network--Clark and Julianne, Doug, and family things in general--Mary could tell that Melissa was struggling with Clark's death and how her sister Julianne was faring, so she was careful to give Melissa room to talk at any length she wanted.

Shortly before they left the restaurant, Mary produced the transfer notice made out to the investment company Ray owned, account number and all. Melissa teared up as she took the transfer paper. "I know you know how much this means to me, and to Ray. He hides it well but he's been feeling kinda low over the past couple months." Her emotion manifested on her face as she reflected on the moment.

"He's such a great guy, Mary... I have to say, I think I'm in love with him. Yes, it's true, I think I want to spend the rest of my life with him! He's been great to me, he's so wonderful with Jamey, and overall just a helluva great guy. And I know that he loves me, I can see it in everything he does; he dotes on me, wants to be with me whenever he can, truly likes being together with me and Jamey. And I can tell in other ways, too, if you know what I mean." She smiled shyly. "He loves this family and is trying desperately to become more involved with all of us."

Mary smiled at her, buffeted by the waves of guilt crashing over her all over again.

Melissa beamed, ignorant of all. "This will be particularly a wonderful gift in his life. His business is faltering a little bit right now and working with our family helps keep him grounded to always realize how lucky he is and how special I am to him." She looked into Mary's eyes and continued, "The more he gets to know our whole family, the more he realizes how lucky he is and how special all of us are to him, each in their own way."

Her wave of guilt falling away with a weird crash, Mary lifted her eyes to gawp at Melissa. Those were the exact words Ray had said to *her*. The exact same! Being an airline attendant, Mary had heard just about every pick-up line there was. She'd witnessed people use the same line two or three times on a single flight, no less. She and her fellow attendants jokingly called these people "the repeaters." Suddenly her mind veered to question: If Ray were really as devoted to Melissa as he claimed, would he be repeating his declarations of devotion with her family members? Her smile faded as a sudden nausea made her sit back suddenly and awkwardly.

"Mary? Are you alright? You suddenly don't look so good."

Mary scrambled to recover. "Oh no, I'm sorry, I'm fine. I just suddenly had a quick wave of nausea. It's gone now, but it hit pretty hard. I hope there was nothing bad in the salad." She laughed and said, "I'm glad things are going well for you and Ray. I don't know him as well as you do, but he seems great. What about his family? Does he have anyone around?"

"No, he was only a child when he lost both his parents. He really never knew any aunts or uncles so he doesn't have any family. I think that's partly why he feels so close to us and wants to be a bigger part of the family."

Mary saw the complete devotion in Melissa's eyes. She dropped the subject in the conversation, but was nowhere near ready to drop it in her own mind.

After a bit more chatter, Mary paid the bill and they walked out together. They would be seeing each other the next day at Julianne's for the family meeting about Clark's service, so the goodbye was brief. Once they'd parted, though, Mary immediately called a friend of hers that did investigative work for her airline and asked him to do a little background research on Ray and his business investment company. Then she called her finance company and put a hold on the transfer until further notice.

CHAPTER 39

Ray stood stock still, boring a hole with his eyes through Jamey's shocked look for a few seconds. Then he broadly smiled at the 10-year-old boy and said, "Jamey! How long ya been standing there?"

Jamey said nothing, paralyzed in his frightened stare.

Ray took a step closer, his broad smile fading like a gesture in inhuman reverse. Jamey started to back away from him but when Ray snapped, "Don't move!" Jamey froze. Ray bent down, staring crookedly face to face with the surprise threat. After a slight calculated hesitation, Ray pulled his head back a tiny distance and continued in an eerily calm and curious tone: "I suppose you heard what I was saying on the phone. Didn't you?" He leaned back in, incrementally, "Well I want to explain, and you need to listen-- and listen real good, understand?" Ending on this tone of warning, Ray leaned in further, his snarling lips now mere inches from Jamey's ear.

Jamey quavered and Ray sneered, unbidden. "I

asked you a question, boy, and I expect an answer. Do – you – understand?" With each syllable his eyes popped. Then his right hand grasped fierce hold of Jamey's left bicep, squeezing hard enough to make the boy winch.

Jamey felt the trickle of warm urine running down his leg.

Ray doubled down in menace: "Well, do you?! I want to hear you use your words." His eyes were now daggers.

Jamey slowly nodded and squeaked out, "Yes."

Ray smiled crocodile wide and jerked his face back suddenly from the boy. He smiled down suggestively, surveying the stain quickly spreading across the front of Jamey's pants, and then down further still, to the small puddle forming on the floor next to the boy's shoe. The smile broadened.

"Relax! That phone call was about a deal I'm working on." He nodded vigorously. "Yeah. A deal that will mean some great things for this family, especially your mother." He probed Jamey's face for reaction but confronted a horrified blank.

He was enjoying it all immensely, emboldened by the risk.

"Now, I admit, my language and some of the stuff

I said is unsavory, but it's just how I have to talk with that prick, who's frankly a real asshole. That means..." he intoned, careening his face closer, "it means... I have to act like an asshole too!" He widened his eyes suddenly, as if to say "boo!" then narrowed them in dead seriousness. "Know what I mean?"

He glared unmoving at Jamey, who was still white with fear and had started to tremble.

"Thing is," Ray drawled, poking a finger at the boy's chest, "your family can't know anything about the deal I'm cooking with this guy."

Jamie trembled and swallowed slowly.

Ray leaned his face down close to Jamey's again, twisting his expression into a threatening sneer as he growled in a new malevolent tone, "They can't know nothing! Especially your mom. You hear me? Nothing!"

Jamey convulsed into sobs, fully unnerved. Ray put a hand on the boys' shoulder, as though to steady him, but his expression didn't alter. "And ... if anyone finds out...people ... might ... get ... hurt. Like your mom. And we wouldn't want that to happen, would we?"

Jamey shook his head and through his sobs said, "No! No..." and lowered his head.

Ray grabbed Jamie by the back of his hair and

jerked it around so the boy was looking back into his glaring eyes.

"Good! And you better fucking remember it... for everyone's sake!" He released his grip on the boy's hair in a gesture of hurling aside something vile, then rose to tower over him. "Now! Go get cleaned up." He shot a glance of warning. "And be sure you wash those pants before your mother gets back, ya baby. She doesn't need to know that her precious little boy pissed his pants. Then stay in your room the rest of the night, reflecting on our sweet little talk." When the boy continued to shake and sob, he ran his hands violently into each of Jamey's pockets, taking his phone and checking for anything else that could prove problematic, then, goose-stepped Jamey to his room to search it as well. Once satisfied that the room was clean of any communicative devises, he slammed the door with a parting scowl and turned off and deposited Jamey's phone into his pocket.

Jamey broke instantly from his spell, throwing himself down on the bed and weeping as quietly as he could into the pillow. His body shook and his stomach did woozy somersaults. Suddenly realizing that he was going to retch, he leaned over the side of the bed just in time to see his school lunch spill over the carpet. Newly horrified, he sat up and quickly grabbed an old sweatshirt to wipe up the vomit as best he could. The last thing he needed was for Ray to be mad about that too.

He stuffed the sweatshirt into the bottom drawer of his dresser, then removed and shoved in his pants too, the patch of urine embarrassingly obvious. He numbly slipped on a pair of sweatpants laying by his bed and sat on the end of it, his mind reeling in fresh frightened tears. If the practice hadn't been cancelled... if he'd only stayed at Billy's instead of having his mom take him home ... But whatever, now what was he supposed to do? He knew for sure he couldn't tell anyone about all this. If he did, Ray would surely hurt him ... or worse. And probably do to the same to his mother! The only thing Jamey knew for sure, even at ten years old, was that whatever Ray was up to, it was not going to be a "*great deal*" for his mom. Or for him, or for anyone else.

Back in the kitchen, Ray cleaned up the pee from the floor, then washed his hands and poured himself a very generous—and deserved-- pour of scotch. Glass in newly steady hand, he reclined in his living room favorite chair that he'd charmed Melissa into buying for him, staring coldly through the sliding glass door down into the courtyard below. A big swallow of the scotch burned pleasantly as it went down and calmed his rising temper. But he couldn't quell the prevailing thought: "*Fuck! Of all the days and all the times the little fucker could have showed up unexpectedly, he had to pick now!"*

But Ray's rage extended to himself as well. Calling his associates from a place with any risk of getting caught was a rookie mistake. Dammit! His furious thoughts focused, wandered, fixed again: *"This changes the whole game. Goddamn it, it was going so good and now I have to take it up a goddamn notch."* The full reality of Ray Allan was surfacing. He swirled his scotch as he angrily calculated his next step.

Suddenly the phone rang. Ray turned his gaze steadily upon the name that came up on the screen and was glad to see it was his associate, ahead of schedule. Why not now answer it in the house, after all that he had been forced to reveal with the boy. The boy, the boy, what would he do with the boy.

"Hello Jackson," he answered emotionlessly.

"Well, howdy there, bossman. I got some primo info on how to get the death money into the checking account."

"Already?" Ray's senses tingled.

"Yeah, it wasn't as tough as I thought it might be. Turns out all that's needed is for her to sign a waiver changing the destination of the death benefit. But that's where it gets a little hairy.

She also has to have a conversation with the insurance company, over the phone, answering questions and verifying that she really wants to change the location. Full disclosure, there also may be some voice recognition involved. However, and calm down now!" He could hear Ray's grunts of displeasure over the line. "However! My guy here, as an expert in this "field," says we could just record a conversation that we use to splice together her words to appease the bank. But. Yes, there's a but. She *will* have to sign a waiver on all this. ... Unless...? Unless we can duplicate her signature."

"How long will all this take to get to a point where we can transfer the money into the account?"

"A week to ten days."
"Then another week to get the funds transferred." Ray gave another short grunt, then sat silent for a minute while he absorbed the information he just received.

"Boss?"

"Yea, I'm here. Another problem has come up. When we talked earlier, that goddamn kid of Melissa's snuck in and was standing here listening to everything we were saying; and I didn't see him. I think he heard the whole conversation, or at least enough it to know that I'm not the good person everybody believes."

"Shit...what'd you do?"

"Well, I literally scared the piss out of him and told him that he would be wise to keep his mouth shut for his and his mother's sake. But we know that doesn't last forever, sooner or later he breaks, or more likely, is that someone notices he's not himself and coerces him to tell them what's wrong. Either way I don't think we have two weeks, maybe two days tops, probably less. We need to figure something out quick and I need to be gone by tomorrow night, I got a bad feeling about this. But I want to try one last tactic for tomorrow. If it works then we can pick up about fifty five grand more along with the 6 grand. I am afraid we'll have to forgo the 300K; I see no way to pull that off, goddamn it. Let me call you back later. I need to think this through, but when I call back you'll have to work fast, we need this wrapped up tomorrow!"

After he hung up the phone he thought about how close he had come to being able to pull off the biggest heist of his career. Thwarted just because of that shit-faced kid! He took another huge swallow of scotch and then, the real Ray was all the way out.

The real Ray Allan was a dangerous, un-caring, murderous psychopath that received pleasure from others' suffering. He sat for about an hour, his anger starting to boil over thinking about his rotten luck and how the kid ought to pay for it when another call came in on his cell phone. He looked at the phone and saw Melissa's name show up on the screen. He took a couple of deep breaths, calmed himself, and reverted back to the charming and dutiful boyfriend. "Hi Baby, how's it going up there?"

"Much better. How are you doing sweetheart? How's it going with Jamey?"

"Oh great. I didn't even have to pick him up. The practice got over early and one of the other kids mother's dropped him off before I left to pick him up. The little bugger surprised me! So we went out and took a walk and played around for a bit. Then had some dinner and he's in his room doing homework now. He said he wanted to turn in early tonight and I said it was a good idea. He looked a little tired. I think everything that has happened has caught up to him, and he misses you. We even talked a little about Clark and Julianne while we walked. Melissa, he is a great kid! Wise beyond his years, I'm lucky to have the opportunity to spend time with him."

Melissa suppressed a tender sob and said, "Thanks Ray, I know he thinks the world of you also. Can I talk to him?"

"Sure, let me get him." Ray put the call on mute, stood up and walked to Jamey's door, stood there for a few seconds, walked back to his chair sat down and un-muted the call. "Meliss...he's asleep. Looks like he did his homework then laid down on his bed and fell asleep in his clothes. I'm going to let him sleep for a while then I'll go in and be sure he gets into bed for the night."

"Oh, OK Ray, be sure and tell him I called and that I love him and I'll see him tomorrow after school."

"You bet I will. I'll take him to school and then what time do want me to come and get you tomorrow?"

"Oh, that's actually why I called. Things have changed for tomorrow. Mary got called into work for a flight tomorrow morning. She leaves around 8AM, so she has already gone home. But she will be back late afternoon. So she suggested that everyone go home in the morning and when she gets back she will pick up Julianne and drive to Doug's house in Salem. Then Allen and Jennifer can come over with the kids and it can be a whole family get together and we all think that will be good for Julianne. She's on board with it all."

Ray made a motion of sticking his finger down his throat and puking, but replied, "That is a great idea! And I agree it will be good for Julianne."

"We all think so too."

"What time do you think you'll be back tomorrow?"

"Probably around noon. We are planning to get up and cook breakfast then take off around 11. So just stay at the apartment and I'll see you then. And…I have some good news for you. Mary is transferring one of her IRA's to you, to the tune of $25,000. Should be in your account tomorrow."

"That's fantastic news Meliss! I am so happy I don't think words could express how I feel. I will have to thank Mary tomorrow at the family get-together. This means so much to me. Listen, since I have the morning free now, I think I will get some more work done. I've been meaning to go see the guy that is interested in some investment advice. Maybe I'm finally on a roll! So if I'm not here right at noonish, don't worry I should be along shortly. Maybe in time for a little alone time before Jamey gets home."

"That sounds delightful!"

"You mean *afternoon delightful*!"

She giggled and said, "Can't wait."

"See you tomorrow, I love you." He hung up the phone, smiled and thought to himself, "*This actually is coming together better than I thought. I was wondering how I could be alone with Julianne tomorrow, and they just solved that for me. When I get her to cooperate tomorrow, and if Mary's transfer gets done early enough...I could be outta here by noon tomorrow with a pretty damn good payload."*

CHAPTER 40

At about the time the after-school conflict between Ray and Jamey was taking place; Salli became agitated to the point of not being able to stay still. Now she paced back and forth in the family room next to the master bedroom where she had slept with Julianne. A part of her wanted to run out and get someone to take her to Jamey, but another part of her said to remain calm and wait. She settled on something in the middle of those two. She went out with the family and stayed on high alert. Constantly watching the window and tilting her head as she received more data.

CHAPTER 41

Ray stayed in the apartment even though he was as anxious as he could ever remember. He purposely waited to call his partner to be sure no one surprised him with an early visit. It'd be just like that horny cow to come traipsing home unexpected. Around 10PM, after confirming the little shit was asleep in his room, he went back to his favorite chair and chanced the call to Jackson to set up the plan for the next day.

"Boss?" Jackson asked.

"Shut up already. I got a plan, so listen close and be sure everyone involved knows exactly where and what their jobs are and that there are no mistakes. We're gunna be cutting this one damn close." He explained the comings and goings of the entire family for the next day before laying out the plan.

"I'll force – I mean "convince" -- the grieving widow to transfer the $55K savings into the checking account tomorrow. Then I'll be able to transfer that and the $6K in the checking to our account that already has the other *investments*. Hopefully another $25K will also transfer into the account from an IRA account that sister-in-law Mary scheduled for tomorrow. So, you need to get a small plane ready to take off tomorrow by noon. Now listen because this is crucial: Have our pilot set up the flight plan to show us leaving an airport in Oregon called Mulino State Airport. It's a little shit-hole town about 20 miles outside Portland and it should be no problem getting in and out of there in seconds. Have the flight plan show us headed to Reno. Of course, I won't be on it. I've got a car stashed and I will head to the Redmond airport. You catch a flight out of Vegas to Portland then Portland to Redmond. I've checked the flights and one leaves Vegas around 9 AM and gets you into Portland around 11AM, then a connecting flight to Redmond leaves at 1:20 and arrives around 2:10. Once I meet you there we'll take off in my stashed car and within 24 hours we'll be out of sight with new identities and new lives." He paused to let his genius sink in, and to luxuriate in it. "Okay? Stay in touch and get it done. Got it?"

"Got it, Boss, see you in about 24 hours. Good luck, get everything you can and be safe." Now Jackson had been a loyal associate of Rays for years. Together they had worked on many shady dealings and both had become dependent on each other. Ray had the charm and brains and Jackson had the muscle and the ability to follow directions, no matter what they were. He always got the job done, regardless of what it was. No questions, no second guessing, just get the job done. Ray knew the importance of having an associate like that, so he always took care of Jackson and over the years they had formed a friendship that was unbreakable. Ray knew his directions would be followed.

"Will do. Goddamn it! This could have gone so much smoother and so much more profitable—that fucking kid! But enough squalling about it, we still are looking at over $100K if all comes together -- let's go get what we can out of it!"

Ray disconnected the call and angrily looked at the time: 10:20. He knew he should get some sleep but he also knew he needed to be at Julianne's house before everyone left her alone for the day. He was guessing they'd all leave the house around 11AM, but he wanted to be there a couple hours before then, just to be safe. He plugged in his phone to recharge it, then, his spidey sense told him to check on Jamey again.

*****

They boy had slept off and on during the time he'd been locked in the bedroom. Being scared out of your mind often results in your body shutting down, after all. Once he'd awoken, he'd tried to think of what to do, but got nowhere.

He considered trying to escape out the window, but it was a long dangerous drop to the ground from the second story, with no bushes or other safe place to land. He sure as hell couldn't overpower Ray, he knew that for a certainty. He had no way of communicating to others, unless he could get the neighbors or someone else on the ground to notice him through the window, and somehow convey a message they'd understand and follow without putting themselves at risk by coming over to the house to investigate.

His mind reeling, young Jamey leaned out the window, trying to scan the courtyard of the apartments next door. He leaned out further, only to feel a strong sudden grip on his leg and a force jerking him back into the room and onto the floor, where he landed in a crumple. Ray Allan stood over him, growling in an almost ecstatic low purr, "Well, you just made my decision a lot easier. I was actually thinking about just letting you sleep through the night, but now, since you decided to be a 'bad boy' I'm going to have to tie you up while I get some shut eye." The boy cowered on the floor, arms covering his head in an unconscious defensive fetal pose.

Ray wanted nothing better than to kill Jamey right then. It would serve the little bastard right after all the trouble he had caused. Still, Ray knew it would be too soon. He knew he needed to postpone the pleasure until just before he left in the morning, just in case something happened during the night that was unexpected. Mommie dearest could call and want to say night-night, or worse yet, actually surprise us with an actual visit, just because she is such a sweet and caring mother. Or that stupid fuck Allen could call with some dumb-ass question. No, better to be safe for the night.

Morning would be fine, it would feel good then too, maybe not as good as right now, but still good, Ray reasoned as he glowered over the huddled mass. Still, what harm could there be in at least letting the little momma's boy know what was in store for him, sooner rather than later? The little fucker deserved at least that.

"Listen, you pathetic worm! I think you should know what's going to happen between us. I'm going to kill you. Yeah, kill you. But not *just* kill you-- I'm going to cut out your heart and stick it in your mouth so your mom can see what a heartless, weak, little wiener you really were."

He grabbed the 10-year-old by the throat and squeezed. Eventually he let out a loud chortle and bound the gasping child to his bed with the materials he had prepared for the job. Duct tape had so many wonderful purposes. For added surety (and pleasure), he grabbed a small hard rubber ball off the nearby dresser and jammed it in the boy's mouth, securing it with piece of duct tape from the roll. Roughly securing it across the boy's quivering lips, he smacked Jamey hard across the face and encouraged him jauntily to breathe through his nose. Shifting his tone to disconcerting and terrifying tenderness, he patted the boy every so softly on the head and said, "Sleep well, lad. I'll see you in the morning." He ominously displayed his watch to the boy. Jamey registered the time as 10:30 and swallowed the tears in his throat as his brain fully registered the deadline for his doom.

CHAPTER 42

Shortly before 5 PM after her lunch with Melissa, Mary received a call from her co-worker who had checked up on Ray. He'd found a Ray Allan registered as a civilian living in Las Vegas, with a listed address. He'd also found that Ray was listed as an independent financial agent. Unmarried, 36 years of age, male, U.S. citizen, no criminal record.

Mary said, "So he's legit?"

The co-worker hesitated. "Well, I wouldn't say that. There is absolutely nothing on him before the 3 years he's been listed in Vegas. And I can't find a social security number for him, at all. Of course he likely has one, so it seems he's going to great lengths to hide it. This has all the signs of an alias, a made-up person, if you will. And another thing, I checked the web page for his investment company and it looks standard, but has no real substance to it. See, generally when a small independent has a company like this, it's tied in to one or more of the large investment brokers, like Prudential, Morgan Stanley, or even

E-trade. Which typically would be listed on the independent broker's web site; in fact, most of the large firms insist on being listed. So I tried to find anyone backing this company, to no avail. I'm going to dig a little deeper tomorrow, but for right now...I'd say beware."

"If he is a phony, how the hell is it he hasn't been caught before?"

"The sad fact is most people don't, or don't know how to, check Like I did. On the surface he looks fine, but once you start a deep check, things can be different. I can't tell you with 100% confidence that he's a fraudster, but I would be very wary to invest with him till we know for sure."

Mary digested the information carefully, asked a couple more questions, then thanked him profusely for his help and hung up, urging him to get back to her right away if he found anything else. She sat for a while thinking about the situation and finally determined that it smelled like three-day-old fish. She got out her phone and called Doug.

"Hi Mary." Doug answered solemnly. "How are you doing?"

"Hi Doug. OK, I guess."

"Yea, I know. This whole situation is bizarre and unbelievable. I wanted to say thank you for coming and being with Julianne. It meant a lot to all of us…"

"Doug." She interrupted, "I need to talk to you. And I would rather just the two of us meet, away from Julianne and Melissa."

"Oh. … Sounds serious. Can you give me a hint?"

"Not over the phone, but can you meet me in a half hour? I was thinking the Grubstake Bar and Grill? It's about 2 miles from Julianne's house on Market Street. Tell Melissa, Alisha, and Julianne some story about needing to get away or something, but come alone."

"Salli is here with me, can I bring her? That's always a good excuse to get away alone for a little while."

"They have a patio, but it isn't the greatest weather to be sitting outside. Oh, I know, there is a park about 6 blocks up on Market past the Grubstake. Meet me in the parking lot and we can just take a walk, keep warm by moving."

"OK, see you in about thirty minutes." Doug hung up wondering what the hell this was all about, but decided that wondering wouldn't help so went to the kitchen where the three girls were having a glass of wine. "Hey ladies, I'm starting to feel like a bit of a slug so I'm going to take Salli out for a walk. I saw a park a couple of miles from here and I think I'll go down there for a while."

Alisha smiled along with Melissa and Julianne, who walked over to give her brother a hug. "Absolutely, go out for a while. You've been the best brother anyone could have ever had. Thank you for everything you've done. I love you."

"You're my sister, you don't have to thank me, and I love you too." He waved at the other two, who were both holding a glass of wine, asking, "Should I stop and get a few more bottles of wine before I return?" He smiled mischievously.

"Maybe four, if you want any for yourself," Alisha retorted with a smile.

He laughed, got Salli in the car and headed to the designated meeting place.

*****

When he arrived at the park, Mary was already waiting. As he let Salli out of the car, the dog rushed over to Mary and gave her a warm welcome. Doug got to them and attached Salli's leash and they took off to walk around the path in the park.

"Thanks for coming so quickly, Doug."

"You bet, it sounded important. So what's going on?"

For the next twenty minutes Mary told Doug her story start to finish, sans the part about sleeping with Ray. She finished by saying, "Doug, I just don't trust him, especially after the info I got from my investigator. I just have a feeling he's not who, or what, he claims."

Doug gave her a serious look and admitted, "I never really trusted him either. I don't know why, but I didn't. So what's next, do you think?"

"Well, the first thing to know is that Melissa is head over in heels in love with him. Trying to convince her without hardcore proof will be next to impossible. We need to be very secretive around her. So I'm thinking we tell Julianne and Melissa that I have a flight tomorrow and that I'll bring Julianne down to Salem so we can all meet about Clark's final arrangement. That way I can talk to Julianne privately while waiting to hear more from the investigator. And you can take Melissa back home. If we find out the worst, then we can confront Ray or even get the police involved."

"Yeah, good plan. So have you and Melissa already put money in his investment company?"

"Yes. I know Melissa has put in all her savings and gives something to him every month. I put in $10,000 and was set to do another $25,000. But I put that on hold till further notice. I don't know if Julianne has done anything, but he's been kissing up to her since Clark's death so I'll find out what I can from her tomorrow. Hopefully afterward we'll have more info to make some decisions."

"OK, so I'm crystal clear: I take Melissa and Alisha back home in the morning after breakfast. We tell Melissa that you had a flight, but that you'll be back in the afternoon to pick up Julianne and bring her down to us. Then the whole family, including the kids, will go to our house for a family gathering. Right?"

"Exactly."

"Hopefully by then we know for sure about Ray and can make some decisions. Alright, let's stay in touch by phone when any information comes in. It's frightening that we don't know what we're dealing with here. If he is a truly bad guy out to bilk the family out of whatever he can, even then we don't know how far-reaching it is. I mean, does he have partners in crime? Is he violent? What has he done in the past? Hell, there are so many possibilities—of course, including the one that he's perfectly legitimate. So let's be extra careful. It would be awful to tar and feather the guy unfairly."

They'd circuited back and were approaching the parking area again. "I agree," Mary said. "Thanks for understanding. I just have a bad feeling..." Doug saw that she was crying.

"Mary, is there something more? Are you okay?

Did something happen?"

She took a deep breath but shook her head and said, "I'm just really nervous about it all...but I'll be fine. Don't worry about me. I'll talk to you tomorrow, just before you leave." She went to her car and left.

Doug decided to walk around the park a bit more with Salli. The last thing he wanted was to raise any suspicions by returning to the women too quickly. Plus, he needed to think on his own for a while.

He appreciated Mary raising her suspicions to him about Ray, and suspected she was probably correct. There was just something about the guy —and he knew Salli sensed it too. He meandered the path deep in thought about his entire family, worried about what the next day would bring. He was so deep in thought, he didn't notice that Salli was watching his every move and absorbing his energy with each new step.

CHAPTER 43

When Doug and Salli arrived back at Julianne's house, he small-talked with the wine-loosened women for a bit, eventually laying out the plans for the next day. Everyone agreed it made sense, and Julianne even commented that it would do her good to get out for a while. They continued chatting in the kitchen for a few minutes, while Salli padded into the front room, stopping and staring out the front picture window.

She tipped her head to one side or the other occasionally, then began pacing back and forth in front of the window. From the kitchen, Alisha eventually noticed the odd behavior and pulled Doug aside.

"Are you seeing this?" She pointed toward the dog. "Something is going on, do you know what could be bothering her?"

"Let's sit down and talk," Doug said cryptically, "but not with the others." He raised his eyebrows in a signal of secrecy.

His wife returned a look of curious acknowledgement, then chimed cheerily to Melissa and Julianne, "Hey you two sisters! Doug and I are going to the store for a couple of things for breakfast. You two keep an eye on Salli, and we'll be back in a few.

Melissa grinned cheekily and said, "I see -- you two need a little 'alone time,' eh?"

Alisha gave a short laugh and said, "If that was the case we'd be back in two minutes."

Doug played along, joking lightly: "You give me too much credit."

The two laughed and waved them away, with Melissa saying she'd use the time to call Ray.

Alisha and Doug took off. As they drove, Doug confided in her all the details of the conversation he'd had with Mary. When they parked at the store, Alisha broke out of her shock and said, "Holy shit, Doug. Do you think this could be true?"

"Unfortunately, yes. Truth is, I never felt comfortable around him, even though, god knows I tried. I even felt odd about it when he was spending so much time here helping out. Did you? But now I'm thinking there may have been a method to his madness. Anyway, it's important not to say anything to Melissa, since she's head over heels in love and probably would vehemently reject any suspicious comments about him."

Alisha nodded in agreement and Doug continued. "So! Mary will talk with Julianne tomorrow after we leave. She should have more info on Ray by then, which she can relay back. Hopefully we'll have some concrete answers by the time the family gathers back at our house. In my heart of hearts, I'm hoping we're wrong about all this and that Ray is the sweetheart he's portrayed to us all…but something tells me that isn't the case. And frankly Salli is practically confirming that by her behavior."

"Yes, Doug. Something is most definitely bothering Salli—it's all coming together! You know, the only times we've ever seen her agitated are when something has been wrong. And she's always agitated around Ray. I have to say, I'm a little scared."

"I know, you're right, so all we can do is stick with the plan we have and keep an extra watchful eye on her, our personal 'divining rod.' Let's see if we can get her to sleep with us tonight. We don't want to cause suspicion, so best not to push it; but let's try."

*****

When they arrived back at the house at around 7PM, they put away the few groceries they'd bought as a cover. While they'd been away, Julianne had made a pot of macaroni and cheese and a green salad. They all tucked in, chatting as they ate and then adjourning to the living room to finish the wine.

The full group couldn't help but notice that Salli seemed preoccupied, but kept up the friendly chatter. Around 10PM, when they all were ready to call it a night, Doug lightly suggested Salli should sleep with him and Alisha since she seemed a bit restless. There were no arguments, especially since Salli was still aloof, looking out the front window.

Everyone else but he and Alisha scattered, but when Doug called out to Salli to come to bed, she was having no part of it. He sat down in the living room with her, while Alisha headed off to their room, hoping Doug could convince her to come to bed. Doug sat, talked to, and petted her, but her high alert never subsided. Doug sat for a while watching her, wondering what was going through her head.

Doug's eyes had become heavy and he even dozed off, but at 10:20PM, Salli became unhinged. Her head jerked up high and she began barking furiously. Doug flew awake and was convinced instantly that something was seriously wrong, and that Salli was now in charge.

CHAPTER 44

After Ray had sufficiently tied Jamey up, he left the bedroom door open and brought over his favorite chair from the living room and planted it near the boy's bedroom door. He poured himself another glass of scotch and sat down, smiling at the thought of the fear that must be coursing through the lad's body and mind. His initial thought of killing Jamey tonight was now replaced with an easy feeling of control. He might, just might, need Jamey tonight for some unknown reason but when he thought about the morning and all it was going to offer, he felt a familiar and satisfying tingle in his groin. Clearly aroused, he sat down at his post with a deep pull of the scotch and soaked up the mental vision of his plan for the next day.

"Should be easy enough. Around 6AM, kill Jamey. Roger that, it'll be fun to have some fun, and that can set the mood for the rest of the day! Then, working on that high, get the burner car, drive to Portland, stalk Julianne's house to be sure everyone leaves. Check! When they've finally all fucked off...go in and force Julianne to transfer the savings account into

checking. Check!

Then transfer all the money from her checking account into my investment account. Check! This was fun indeed! *Then...kill Julianne? Maybe, that would be fun also, of course, and she probably wants to join old Clarkie boy anyway.* His mind caught on some new dark thought, and his eyes narrowed. *But... maybe not though ... might be more fun to know just how much she can suffer.*

He sat motionless in the shadows, a snarl climbing darkly over his upper lip as he relished the thought of relishing her pain, however far he might extend it before she passed out. This went on a while before his mind moved on to the final stage of the plan. *After that, a leisurely trip to Redmond and pick up Jackson. Check! And finally, blissfully out of this whole bloody mess! Checkmate!"*

But before the beautiful conclusion to this long lovely grift, he'd get his beauty rest. There wasn't even a need to set an alarm since he knew his subconscious--so fixed on the glorious plan--would rouse him well before it was time to head out to put it all in motion. He savored the rest of his scotch (and the rest of another, pre-celebratory, dram), laid his head back against the chair and swam in the enjoyment of the anticipation. It was all so intoxicating that he even enjoyed a quick wank in the comfy chair before falling to contented sleep.

CHAPTER 45

Alarmed by the urgent barking, three women burst quickly out of their rooms. Salli continued her ear-blasting alarm.

"Doug, what's wrong?" yelled Alisha. She had not yet fallen asleep, so had been the first to return to the living room.

"I don't know, but clearly something's happened!" Alisha ran to his side and clasped his sweaty hand.

Melissa came out of her room, hastily wrapping a robe around her. "What's going on?!" she cried groggily.

Salli ran directly to her and started barking at her in a demanding fashion that further startled everyone. Melissa stumbled back till the wall stopped her. "What the hell is going on?!" Just then Salli grabbed Melissa's robe in her jaws and began to pull Melissa toward Doug. Melissa shrieked and snatched the robe away from the aggressive canine.

Salli released her grip instantly and trotted back

to Doug, but there she began the barking all over again. Doug suddenly understood that she was trying to convey that something had happened *out there* that had to do with Melissa *in here*.

He sputtered, "She wants you and me to go with her! Something is going on and, knowing her how I do, I know we'd best follow her lead."

"Something happened?" Melissa screamed. "What in hell are you raving about, Doug!?" By now Salli had barked her way to the back door, which led to the driveway. She then fell insistently silent as she stared urgently at Melissa and Doug. Melissa started to cry.

"Sis, it's okay, I promise! Get some clothes on; I think she's saying we need to drive her somewhere, and I have a sneaking suspicion that 'somewhere' is your apartment. Just trust me and hurry! I'll get the car, meet me there as quick as you can!"

"*My* house! What the hell could be at *my* house that would cause her to do this?!"

"Melissa, listen, it's all going to be okay. I don't know precisely what's going on...but I do know to listen when she talks. So hurry quick and meet me at the car!"

After she pivoted and hustled toward her bedroom, he turned to Alisha. "Look, you've gotta get hold of Mary and get her over here right away. Tell Julianne the story I told you today, and then stay put till you hear from us."

He turned to hug his other sister, assuring her quietly, "I know. I know this is confusing and frightening, and I hope I'm wrong about it all, but we have to be sure." He held her shoulders reassuringly and looked her in the eye. "Everything will be fine, trust me. Just listen to Alisha, and I'll call just as soon as I know anything more." He gave her another hug before releasing her, then looked at Alisha and said, "Don't let anyone in here except Mary. No one. You got it?" Alisha wiped away a tear, soberly nodding, then quickly gave him a confidence-boosting kiss. Next thing they all knew he was out the door and the car was running. Salli waited stock still until Melissa was ready, then shot out the door and they both jumped into the car.

*****

At the rate Doug was driving, it took only about five minutes to get on the freeway headed south to Salem. Salli sat in back, her head poised intently between the bucket seats, her gaze fixed on the road ahead.

Melissa dialed Ray Allan's cell phone but got no answer, so she left him a stern voice mail message instructing him to call as soon as possible. She then called Jamey's phone, which went immediately to voice mail, which she knew meant that his phone was off. She left a message for him too. Then she shot a helpless look at Doug and said, "How do we know we are going the right way, or to the right place?"

"She'd let us know otherwise." He tipped his head toward Salli.

"Are you sure, Doug? I mean, what if she just doesn't know we're headed the wrong way."

"Trust me, she'd know."

Anxiously, Melissa tried Ray's phone again and left another message. Then almost immediately did it again, and then again. Doug's fingers ached; he was grasping the steering wheel so tightly. Salli's fixed look ahead never wavered.

When they finally pulled into the apartment complex's parking lot at 11:10PM, Melissa darted out of the car before it had even come to a full stop, lurching a bit as she slammed the car door and raced up the stairs toward her second floor apartment. Sallie had managed to bullet out the door before the crazed woman had hurled it closed, and sped after her, with Doug following closely behind.

*****

Ray Allan snapped awake with a start, his back and neck aching from the slumped position he'd fallen into on watch. *Shit!* He quickly looked at his watch: 11:10PM. He knew something had awoken him, but wasn't sure what it had been. He reached to his pocket for his phone ... but it wasn't there. His mind reeling fast back into heightened focus, he remembered: he'd left it in the living room to recharge. Another rookie mistake! What had he been thinking?! He immediately was angry at himself. What if he'd missed a call that jeopardized his perfect plan?

He darted a glance at the bound boy in his bed to ensure he was still properly subdued, then rushed to the living room. *Fuck!* Four missed calls and, more ominously, four new voice mails--all from Melissa. *Fuck!* Stabbing at the screen to quickly play the first message, he blanched. They were in route to the apartment. Based on the time of the message, it was nauseatingly clear: They could be here any second.

He sprinted to the kitchen and grabbed the largest knife. Racing back to Jamey's room, he frantically began to cut the boy free from the tape that held him down. He was just starting to remove the tape from Jamey's mouth when he heard the front doorknob rattle. Locked, ha! Still, knowing what would come next while hoping blindly that it wouldn't, he stood frozen with his ears cocked. Sure enough, was that the scrape of an ill-fitting key sliding into the deadbolt? *Fuck!*

*****

As soon as Melissa turned the knob, Salli pushed her way in and ran to Jamey's open bedroom door. The dog's face was contorted into a vicious and frightening snarl, emitting a steady, low, menacing growl. Doug and Melissa ran up alongside of her, panting at the effort but quickly going white at the sight they beheld. Fear replaced adrenaline coursing through their bodies, and their temples pulsed to punctuate the heartbeats pounding in their ears. There, just inside the threshold of the room, stood Ray Allen, smirking defiantly, gripping Jamey in front of him with an arm viced around his neck. The young boy was gagged with duct tape. Ray was lightly caressing the boy's temple with a long, sharp, serrated carving knife. Doug and Melissa gasped in horror.

*****

After hearing the doorknob rattle, Ray's mind had raced as he darted to the bed, where the child's eyes bulged up at him.

If he tore the tape off the boy's mouth and jerked the ball out, could he act like nothing was wrong? He could say Jamey had called out from a nightmare (ha!) and that conscientious Ray was checking on him--simple as that. The boy looks disturbed because he's scared from the dream, and not yet able to register it as a bad dream.

But no! Ray quickly dismissed that course. The boy was still in his clothes and it was clear from the stench that he'd pissed himself again. Plus the boy could be too easily convincing that the "nightmare" was all too real. So he left the ball and tape in place and jerked the boy up, spinning him around to face the door as he lifted the glistening knife to the child's trembling head.

He knew this threatening posture would stop Melissa and whoever else was with her in their tracks. But he hadn't expected the goddamn dog.

As Salli burst into the doorframe, Ray was just yanking him out of bed. Salli snarled, planted in the doorway, shaking her hips in readiness to pounce, but just then Ray twirled the boy around, protecting him from her planned attack. Twirling next into the dog's view was the gleaming steel of the knife blade, as Ray traced a dastardly circle 8 around the boys eyes and ears and the soft skin in between. Salli's brain signaled her to stop moving, but her growl continued, even as Melissa and Doug finally caught up to her.

Ray's face stretched into a repulsive smile as his eyes fixed coldly on Melissa. He cheerily said, "Meliss! My darling! I know you don't want to see your precious little boy with this knife planted in his ear and his brains leaking out all over his nice shirt." She burst into sobs and threw her hands over his face. "Good, then might I kindly suggest you get control of that growling cur and of course your big oh-so-brave brother there." Doug was playing it as cool as he could, following Salli's lead to watch and wait.

"Ray?! ...What are you...? ... Why is this ha...? I don't under...Why??!!" She stood dumbstruck looking at Ray holding her phone in her hand.

Ray shook his head as though surveying a stupid animal, snatched the phone from her hand, then his grin curled further in mockery. "Blea...blea..blu..duhhh...Jesus Christ, you stupid fuck. You never were worth a shit in any kind of crisis...or come to think of it, ever at all." Melissa sobbed louder. Ray chuckled and panned his stone-cold smile methodically to Doug, dancing the blade ever playfully around Jamey's temple. A new urine stain was spreading down the boy's leg.

"So! Shall we safely assume the fight's going to fall to you, big brother?" He jabbed lightly at the corner of Jamey's eye with the blade, grinning at Doug whose blood pounding in his own temple gave way to the sound of the child's low hopeless moan. He stood up straighter, keeping his expression as blank as he could.

Ray basked in the scent of fear billowing like a cloud in the room. "You smell that? It's the odorous mix of this prick's piss, his useless mother's tears, and your pathetic fear!" He made a dramatic gesture of sniffing up the air around him, but kept his eyes fixed on Doug, glaring down his arrogant nose at him.

"You're probably used to her spinelessness, knowing the worthless cunt your whole life. What a sad bastard you are. So, how about you do me a kindness, do something worth a shit for a change and get control of your mewling sister and that irritating dog!"

Doug couldn't control the rage from rising in him. He realized his hands had become fists and his body was tensing for a strike only when Ray laughingly admonished him with a more determined poke of the knife into his nephew's nostril. "Uh uh uh, not so fast there, little Dougie." He twisted the edge of the blade back and forth in the tender flesh of Jamey's nose, drawing forth a trickle of blood. "Trust me Doug, you dimwitted mutt. I will brain him before I kill him, and only just before I kill the rest of you mongrels. This isn't my first dog fight, fucker. I'm getting out of this, and the quicker you come to understand that, the better it will be for you and your whole dog-chow-chugging family." Salli's hackles rose higher on her back and her growl deepened, even as she remained motionless. Doug loosened his fists. Melissa and Jamey shook with silent sobs. Ray slowly pushed everyone out of the bedroom and into the kitchen, making sure that Salli moved so as not to get an opportunity to make an attack.

"So here's what going to happen, fucko. I'm taking the kid and Melissa with me. Think of it as my very own insurance policy to get away. What you need to do is this…quiet your goddamn dog and sit like a good boy, right here. If you can behave like good dogs and refrain from barking for the cops, then soon enough I'll let you know where to retrieve these two pieces of shit. Unharmed, naturally." His terminal joker grin vanished in an instant. "Then you can have your precious family back and try to patch up the damage that big bad Ray did."

Doug nodded as benignly as he could. "Okay, Ray, I hear you. And I want to help end this without trouble for anyone, I promise. You can tie us all up and just take off without the annoyance of hysterical hostages. No one would possibly come looking for us until tomorrow. That will give you the whole night to get far far away from here."

The corners of Ray's mouth turned up slightly. "Do you promise, Doug?"

Doug extended his hands, wrists crossed as if waiting to be bound. "Yes, Ray. I promise." Sallie's ear twitched ever so slightly.

Ray guffawed and everyone jumped. The knife

played dangerously around Jamey's cheek as the belly laugh continued. When he finished, his back straightened sharply and he repositioned the knife handle in his palm. "Jesus, you must think I'm stupid as a shithouse rat. Nice try, Dougie, but I'll take my insurance policy along with me. It's my business after all, and I have to trust my own expert advice."

In a flash he flipped the knife in his hand and lunged forward, choking Jamey in the crook of his other elbow as he swiftly and accurately bashed the handle of the knife into the tissue just under Melissa's left eye, before returning to his previous stance. Jamey gurgled for air beneath the duct tape as Melissa screamed in a shock of pain.

"That's just so you remember who's in charge, bitch!" At this Salli finally barked, taking a step closer to Ray as she did so. He immediately turned the blade horizontally to the boy's neck and turned his ugly gaze to the dog, saying softly: "Go ahead, you...fucking... mutt. Just try it. If you want me to gut this fucker like a fish!" Salli cocked her head slightly but stayed still and stopped growling. She stared, seemingly quizzical, into Ray's eyes. Ray then flashed a crooked grin as if fantasizing all the different ways he could cause pain to Doug's precious dog and the rest of them—he smiled, as one thought crept into his mind.

Salli shifted closer to Doug and sat down suddenly, tilting her head ever so slightly to the other side. Doug shot a glance down at her and realized instinctively that she had *seen* something in that moment. He kept his expression blank and returned it to the madman who held the knife to his nephew's young neck.

Just then Ray lunged forward again, purposely choking the boy as he used the last three fingers of the knife-wielding hand to snatch Melissa by the hair. He twirled her hair around for a secure hold and jerked her toward him, snarling, "Listen Meliss, my *darling*. You're going to do as I say, whenever I say it, or your darling little boy here..." – without moving his eyes from Melissa, he gestured to the cowering child with a violent new squeeze of his elbow – "...dies right in front of you." The boy's mother howled into her wet trembling hands, her hair pulling sharply in Ray's grasp.

Ray turned his eyes to her brother: "Don't worry, Doug, I know just how to help you be a good doggie too. Melissa, quit your bawling and go get our special handcuffs from your bedroom." He didn't look at her when he ordered this, untwisting her hair from his fist lasciviously, but raised a jaunty eyebrow at Doug while he did it, whispering, "Who knew they'd be good for something else." She gasped in embarrassment and sobbed anew, but when Ray lifted her son's head up by the jaw with the sharp end of the knife blade and said, "Look, boy, at how useless your whore mom is!" She swore her allegiance and hurried off to get the cuffs.

"You bastard," Doug said under his breath, then more vehemently: "You hurt either of them and I'll kill you!"

"oooooh, I saw that movie too. Now hand over your phone! 'Die Hard?'" Ray mocked as he slid the blade up and down Jamey's neck waiting for Melissa's sniffling return.

He then commanded Melissa to handcuff Doug to the solid metal door handle of the oven. As she did, Ray smashed Doug's cell phone with the base of the knife. Doug's mind whirred, knowing there was no landline. Ray then roughly tore the tape off Jamey's mouth and, with a hard slap on alternate cheeks with each word, warned him "Not. To. Make. A. Single. Fucking. Sound," allowed the child to spit out the rubber ball. After he did so, Jamey heaved to catch his breath but held his tongue. The knife was perched at the base of his skull now, tickling his brainpan.

Ray removed it for a moment to stab in the direction of the snot- and saliva-covered ball on the floor, instructing Doug in an incongruously sweet voice to "fetch the ball, doggie, and shove it down your own goddamn throat." Doug didn't give him the satisfaction of shuddering, but calmly kneeled, collected the ball and placed it into his mouth, gagging slightly as he closed his mouth around the soggy object.

Ray continued his deceptively dulcet tone. "Alrighty, then, good boy! Now, Meliss, my sweet, kindly fetch that duct tape from the nightstand in the bedroom and tape his bullshit mouth closed, please. Then bind his hands nice and tight around the cuffs with tape too." She did as instructed, stifling sobs as tears streamed down her face.

"Good bitch, good obedient bitch," he muttered as she completed the task. "And now for the next stupid pet trick: Restrain that goddamn dog that you all seem to love and trust you so much! Wrap her vicious snout with duct tape and tie all her legs together with that long leash there in the living room, so I don't have to look at her stupid face anymore." He jabbed the knife toward the retractable-cord leash Jamey kept on a hook by the front door for the happy days when Salli visited and he got to go on walks with her. She obeyed through heaving sobs, attaching the leash to her collar, taking her into the living room, wrapping up her legs and then attaching the leash to the leg of the heavy couch in the living room. Ray took a brief look at the job she had done and was satisfied.

"Good, well done, you did something right for a

change, you stupid bitch. You're lucky I didn't just kill the dumb cur but I wouldn't want anyone to think I'm the anti-Bob Barker or anything, now would I? I have a reputation to uphold after all." (The truth was he harbored a superstition he couldn't quite put his finger on about how killing the animal could make for bad luck for himself down the line. With that eerie look she kept giving him, she seemed half ghost already!)

He then had Jamey duct-tape his mother's mouth and hands, then did the same again to the boy. Hogtied and handcuffed to the oven with his beloved Salli suffering the same fate in the next room--Doug now watched from a skewed slantwise vantage as Ray took turns jabbing at his sister's and nephew's backs, goose-stepping them to the front door, and out of the house-- to god knew where the cursed night, and cursed grifter, might lead them.

CHAPTER 46

Ray fished Melissa's car keys out of his pocket, activated the cheery double-bloop to unlock the vehicle's back seat and shoved her into it. He jammed Jamey down in the passenger seat and held the knife to his ribcage as he drove with the other hand. He drove the short distance to the 'burner' car he'd bought and stashed some time ago--of course using one of the stupid woman's credit cards.

He transferred his "insurance" to the burner car gruffly, holding the knife to the 10-year-old's neck to encourage his mother to climb into the trunk. After then shoving the boy into the passenger seat, he drove it out to the street and then locked the boy in while he jogged back and hid Melissa's car in the woody hidey place the burner had previously occupied, to ensure it wouldn't be spotted. He then veritably *skipped* back and hopped back into the driver's seat of the burner car. Cheerful as a child at the rodeo, he flashed a happy grin at the boy, sitting stock still in terror beside him. "That's a good boy. What a good dog, just be sure you stay that way." The smile, along with all giddy energy, drained from his face and body as he pulled back onto the main road, the streetlights illuminating half his face like a skeleton. Pulling out Melissa's phone and Jamey's phone, he tried to think of what the next hour or so would bring. Then turned Jamey's phone on again, so that both phones were operational. He whistled tunelessly as he headed for his final destination-- well, at least the final destination for this stupid family.

It was 12:02AM.

*****

As soon as the door was closed, Doug started investigating the handcuffs for a way to get out of them. He started to pull at the oven door handle to see if by chance the handle was loose. He saw quickly it wasn't so he started thinking of other alternatives. His eyes darted around the kitchen wildly looking for tools and saw Jamey's "handyman in training" toolbox (ironically, a gift from Ray to ingratiate himself further to the boy and family) on a shelf in the far corner of the room. Eternally out of reach!

His mind was racing for ideas when suddenly Salli was there beside him. "Oh my god! Hello you brilliant girl!" He said through his taped mouth.

She had somehow wrangled out of the leash

Melissa had wrapped around her legs and easily broke the cord at the clasp of the leash that was attached to her collar.—Perhaps Ray hadn't bothered to check how "securely" she'd been bound in the next room. Her snout was still wrapped with duct tape but she was clearly there to help.

She gave Doug a tail wag and a quiet whine, as she pawed at the tape restraining her mussel. "Come here," Doug gestured with his chin and she shimmied down to place her snout beneath the oven handles. This put his fingers in range to worry at the tape till he finally got it unwrapped.

Salli barked a single bark of thankful freedom, and quickly Doug pushed his taped face to her and she instantly understood. He leaned in and allowed her to gently lick and bite at the tape till she was able to peel off the strip. He immediately spit out the ball and cried, "Good girl! Now let's get me out of these cuffs!"

She bit down on the oven door handle and started to pull down on it but they both could see it would be a futile effort. "Wait, stop, Salli. We need something else. Oh, the toolbox!" He thought through the needed steps and said to her, "Salli, first get the tape off my hands." He wiggled them and made an exaggerated chewing motion with his mouth; immediately she began to bite at the tape around his wrists. After just a few seconds she'd carefully torn through enough of the tape with her teeth that Doug was able to free his right arm. He then pointed straight to the toolbox: "Salli, get the toolbox!" She paused, her head tilted attentively!" Salli didn't seem to understand so Doug focused inwardly on the thought, screaming it in his mind while looking directly at her. Suddenly, her head jerked toward the toolbox and she grabbed the handle and sprinted the toolbox back to Doug. Doug grinned at her in astonishment, "Way to read my mind, girl!"

With his now free hand he took the hammer out and pounded on the left side of the oven door. It didn't dent easily, but eventually he'd smashed enough damage around the handle casing that he could get the claw of the hammer under the loosening screws and pry it loose through a series of adrenaline-fueled shouting heaves. "Haha!" Doug slipped the loop of the cuffs free from the handle and reached immediately to hug Salli.

He beamed at her, scuffing her lovingly behind both ears, which caused the remaining handcuff loop to lightly thump up alongside her head. His gaze focused from joy to understanding quickly: "You know something, don't you, Salli? You know what this bastard is up too!" She instantly started wagging her tail like a hummingbird, barking and pulling Doug to the front door by the cuffs. He grabbed some duct tape and taped the loose handcuff to his left arm to prevent the dangle and jangle then stumbled down the stairs following her and within seconds the two were on the ground floor sprinting to the car.

By this time the ruckus had awakened a few neighbors and some were standing outside their apartments at a safe distance, cautiously surveying the situation. One of them recognized Doug as he darted forward, gasping: "Doug! What's happening?"

Doug was thrilled to see a familiar face and they stopped for a second. "No time to explain," Doug panted as he straightened his back to the quickly evolving emergency. "Call the police and tell them it's a matter of life and death but they must call me on your phone before they do anything else!" He jabbed out his left hand, the cuffs visible from the gesture.

Luckily the neighbor knew him well and trusted Doug implicitly. Still, this was all quite the shock. "*My* phone!"

"Yes! I don't have time to explain but I need it, *right now*!"

The man nodded, snatched his phone from his bathrobe pocket and jerked it over to Doug. He was panting now too. "I don't know what the hell is going on, but here you go! I'll call the police from my landline right now!" Salli took the cue and continued her sprint to the car, with Doug keeping pace right behind her. He quickly unlocked the vehicle and Salli dove across the driver's seat into the passenger position the moment he opened the door.

As he sped out to the main street, he noted the time: 12:38AM. He stopped, not knowing exactly where he was going. Back to Portland? To his house? Allen and Jennifer's? He looked at the focused dog and said, "Where're we going Salli!?" She gave him a knowing look, then instead of pointing her snout in any particular direction, squatted down and lay her head down on the seat, turning it sideways to smile happily while wagging her tail. Doug knew immediately: This was Salli's pose whenever they were headed home to see Alisha. He shouted, "Alisha!" and as soon as Salli heard the name she jumped back up and faced forward in the seat, barking in approval and urgency.

Since Alisha was at Julianne's house, Doug headed straight there. He knew that Salli knew her exact whereabouts too. Just then the borrowed cell phone rang. He jabbed at the answer button as he accelerated into a turn. It was the Salem Police Department. An officer was calling from the scene. "This is Doug!"

"Hello. This is Officer Ryan Morris of the Salem

Police. We were told you could shed some light on what's going on here."

"Yes sir, I can." And for the next 5 minutes Doug told the story of Melissa and Ray Allan to Officer Morris. Just as he got to the part where he was telling him about where he was going and why, the line went dead. Doug pulled it back to glimpse the dreaded dead-battery icon before the screen went fully dark. "No, No, No... NOoooo. You got to be fucking kidding me!!" He pounded at the power button to no avail, aghast at the knowledge there was no charger in the car. "Fuck!" Salli gave him a steady glance, then turned her head forward again. He threw the useless device the floor, saying, "I get it, I get it! No time to stop now!" He looked at his watch: 12:50AM.

CHAPTER 47

Mary made it to Julianne's house around 11:15PM. Alisha greeted her sister, then sat her down with Julianne and had Mary go through the entire story as she knew it. After the story was over and a few questions were asked, Julianne blanched. "Oh shit you guys; I've got him as a signer on my checking account!"

"What?" Alisha cried. "Why, for Christ's sake?!"

Julianne looked shell-shocked. "Well, it's just that Melissa was really encouraging me to do it and quite frankly he was so sweet to me and said he had experience doing this for other people. I thought it would be a good way to include him in the family and quite frankly I didn't want to deal with the crap he said he was dealing with. It seemed like the right thing to do." She turned her eyes in shame to the floor and looked about to cry.

Mary jumped in. "Hold on a second, both of you. We don't know for sure what's going on yet. We are just theorizing right now." The other two women looked at her agog but she continued.

"We could be all wrong. Let's wait for Doug to call. He's on the case, we know, and it shouldn't be too long before he checks in."

Alisha went to and hugged Julianne and said, "Sorry I snapped, I'm just a little on edge." She kissed her on top of her head and then went and got the remainder of the wine. She poured three glasses, and they all sat in the living room discussing their respective concerns about Ray Allan, trying to stave off the smell of anxiety that grew in the room each second the phone didn't ring and the door didn't open.

Around midnight Alisha admitted, "I'd have thought we'd have heard from Doug by now. I mean, he and Melissa have been gone more than an hour by now." The eyes of the other two brimmed with tears of concern, loosened further by the wine. Not wanting to ratchet up more worry than was warranted, Alisha quickly added: "But! He and Melissa may just be taking care of Jamey, so let's not freak them out more than we need to, and just remain patient." Julianne and Mary nodded numbly.

The seconds ticked past at a glacial pace, and when an eternal fifteen more excruciating minutes had crept past, at 12:15 Alisha knew she shouldn't wait any longer, come whatever may. The others were growing inconsolably hopeless. She called his cell number and it went immediately to voice mail. She left a message that said to call her back ASAP. "That's not like Doug; why would he shut his phone off? He never does that!"

Julianne said, "Why don't I call Melissa? She may know what's going on." But after four rings, Melissa's phone also went to voice mail. Julianne also left a message to get back to her ASAP, and hung up with a look of true worry. She looked at Alisha and said, "This seems extra strange, for both phones to go to voice mail, right?"

They tried both phones again: voicemail again both times. Their joint fear was climbing. Then Julianne shouted, "Jamey! He has a phone of his own!" and quickly dialed it: It rang but voicemail there too. Now all three women were pacing in their worry and distraught uncertainty. Suddenly Julianne froze in place, looked at the other two and said, "Wait! I have Ray's phone number! Should I call him?" Mary and Alisha returned looks of fear, but Alisha quickly said, "Yes, do it. If he answers you can bluff something, but if we get his voicemail too, then that's a sign something truly is wrong." Mary gulped but nodded slowly in agreement, and so Julianne dug up and dialed Ray's number.

It rang twice, then Ray answered.

Julianne's eyes popped and she gulped audibly. The other two women immediately huddled around her in a group hug to lend strength and be sure to hear every word.

"Julianne! What in the world are you doing awake at this hour. You should be sleeping, young lady." He said sternly with what was now clearly to her ears a fake laugh. She calmed herself as the others gave her "you can do this" looks as they tightened the three-way physical bond between themselves.

Julianne put on a casual tone. "Hi Ray! It's just, we're all were getting a little concerned over here."

"Concerned?"

"Yes. It may sound silly but Doug and Melissa left about 2 hours ago to go to Melissa's. The dog suddenly went nuts and seemed to want Melissa to go back home for some reason. Have you seen them?"

"Oh, it's all good. Yeah, they arrived some time after eleven, I'd guess. They actually woke me up from my beauty sleep, ha! They apologized for showing up so late and told me about Salli's weird fit. Strange dog, isn't she? The only thing we could figure was that Jamey wasn't feeling very well earlier and maybe she 'sensed' it? But everything is fine. That crazy dog must be getting a little too protective. We're just about to your place. Hasn't Doug called you?"

"No, and Alisha is a bit concerned. She's tried calling him and his phone seems to be off, it goes directly to voice mail." Mary and Alisha turned both their suddenly sober heads toward her with the same quizzical look that had emerged from her own face. She took a breath. "Wait, you said *you're* almost here?!" The three women embraced each other a bit more tightly.

"Yea, I am. I thought Doug was calling to update you but maybe I got my wires crossed. Doug decided to stay in Salem with the dog because she just wasn't settling down. He said he was headed home because she might be able to chill better there. His idea was they'd get better sleep there and it'd give him a chance to check in on work tomorrow. But never fear, the plan is still for us all at his place tomorrow. Melissa felt compelled for her and Jamey to come back to be with all of you, so I offered to take em. Huh, not sure why he didn't call--maybe his phone died?"

At the word "died," the triad of women's backs straightened as one. Julianne maintained her breezy tone: "Oh, got it! So, Melissa and Jamey are with you?"

"Yep, Meliss conked out in the backseat but Jamey just woke up and is right here next to me. Jamey...say hi to your Aunt Jules."

"Hi Aunt Jules."

"Hi Jamey. Sounds like you've had a big day."

"Yea."

"Also sounds like you'll be here in a few minutes."

"Yea, I guess."

His tone was odd; hackles rose on the back of all three motherly necks: "Are you OK honey?"

"Yea."

Then suddenly Ray was back on and laughingly interrupted. "Poor kid ain't much for chatter tonight, I guess. It's been a long day and he's about as tired as his mom seems to be. Anyhoo, we'll be there in a few, and then I can help you see about connecting with Doug to make sure he's okay too. See you shortly." Abruptly, the call ended.

Julianne put the phone down slowly as the three split from their hug into a loose triangle of defiant moms beneath the glare of the kitchen lights. Julianne spoke first. "Sooo? Ray will be here, in this house, in a few minutes. And he's pretty sure Doug just randomly decided to stay in Salem and can't check in with us b/c his phone lost its charge?"

"Yeah, that's all total bullshit!" Alisha shouted what all three were feeling in joint angry fear.

CHAPTER 48

Ray heard Melissa's phone ringing from his back pocket, and then Jamey's rang also, safely in Ray's front pocket. He figured he'd be the next call. Right on cue, he smiled down at his vibrating phone to see Julianne's name showing on the screen. The timing was perfect: He turned off the headlights and pulled up to Julianne's house unseen as he answered the call. He parked on the street a bit beyond the driveway to remain unnoticed. This positioned him for a quick getaway if needed too. From the darkness of the sedan he repositioned the knife at the kid's ribcage and looked back at the house to be sure no one had seen anything.

All looked perfect. As he continued the conversation with Julianne, he casually pulled a Glock 9 handgun out from under his seat and replaced the knife pointed toward Jamey. Setting the phone between his left shoulder and cheek, he continued talking while giving the kid a "don't even" look as he kept the gun pointed at him, checking the clip of bullets and then shoving them into position—careful to make each gun move when the volume of his confident voice would veil the sound. As he continued to lie blithely to Julianne, he quietly and slowly pulled back the barrel, cocking the hammer and loading the first bullet from the clip into the chamber, keeping it aimed at the trembling 10-year-old at every step.

Jamey's eyes revealed new depths of horror as Ray now raised the gun and placed the cold metal against the boy's sweaty head. Ray chirped into the phone, "Jamey, say hi to your Aunt Jules," as he pressed the gun even harder against the tender skin and mouthed silently, slowly and viciously: "Do. it. perfect." He removed the tape from his mouth and moved the phone in front of Jamey's mouth as he tapped the barrel of the gun against his temple and gestured knowingly back over his shoulder, to the trunk where Melissa lay trapped.

Ray was proud that he remembered the stupid nickname Jamey used with Julianne. Just one more schmaltzy family sentiment he'd suffered through but was now putting to his advantage. He knew he'd have to move quickly as soon as he hung up, but having the kid talk was a nice touch that might gain him a second or two.

As soon as Ray had pulled the phone back from the kid (right as the little shit looked about to cry) and wrapped up the call satisfactorily, he sprung out of the dark car, hurried around to jerk Jamey out of the passenger seat, and hauled the whimpering simpleton to the front door with his left elbow crooked around the quivering neck and the pistol in his right hand, down at his hip for discretion. He took the spare key he'd acquired from Melissa's purse and slid it silently into the lock. Pausing for a few seconds as he lifted the gun back to the boy's head on the dark doorstep, he grinned when he heard Alisha shout, "Total bullshit!" Guards were clearly down. He couldn't have asked for a better cue! He quietly turned the key, then used the same left hand to turn the knob as he kicked open the door and shoved the boy in before him at gunpoint.

The three women turned with a start at the sound of a powerful smash—and there Ray was, standing in the entryway, Jamey in a vice grip in front of him--with a gun held to his head. Julianne threw her hands to her face in a shrill scream. Mary and Alisha gasped in horror. All three stood stock still for a moment, staring in disbelief at the unbelievable scene playing out before them.

Ray's face was all grin. "Well well well, good evening ladies! Oh! Actually it's morning now, isn't it? I'm so terribly sorry to interrupt your 'wining.' I hope you've all had as wonderful a day as Jamey and me...Isn't that right, Jamey-boy, hasn't it been a hoot?" Jamey slumped red-faced and silently weeping in the grip of Ray's tightly squeezing arm. His youthful face was covered in tears, sweat, dirt and snot and he now broke out into a trauma-induced moan.

"Awww, was it. not. your. favorite. day. then?" Ray bounced the gun barrel on the child's temple with each mocking syllable, then pushed it in hard and shot his menacing smirk over to the women. "Thanks for having us! I just thought; why not make one last lovely visit before I depart for parts unknown once more." He kicked the door closed behind him without shifting his gaze, then jerked the boy forward as he took a huge stride closer to the women. "Wasn't that *thoughtful* of me?!"

The women managed to remain calm as they subtly shifted closer to each other again. They were standing shoulder to shoulder with palms raised beseechingly when Julianne managed to utter, "Where's Melissa?"

"*Asleep in the car.* Well, a part of the car." He chuckled. "I didn't want to *wake her*; you know what a very considerate fellow I am." He smiled a newly devious smile and then suddenly shifted tone, saying in a brisk businesslike tone: "Now! Down to business." He strode forward another long step, choke-shoving Jamey ahead of him. The boy stumbled so he kneed him in the ass and twisted the gun roughly between his jawbone to get him to stand back up straight. Still the little coward couldn't stop shaking in silent tears so he rapped the gun once sharply into the underside of his jaw, saying harshly—without looking down at the child—"What are you bawling about, boy?!" But just as quickly his eyes renewed their luster. "Now, ladies! I am here for a very specific purpose and the quicker we can get this done the quicker I will leave you so you can enjoy the rest of your day."

Mary spoke next: "Listen, Ray..."

Ray cut her off with a snarl. "Shut up, you! I have a feeling *you* were part of the *unfortunate complications* I'm dealing with here, so you probably want to keep me calm." He paused, giving a little arrogant upward twitch of the head before lowering his brow and continuing in a conspiratorial whisper: "In fact, I think *all* of you will want me to help me stay calm. ... Because ... if I become at all agitated ... you know ...?" He hesitated again, then screamed as he smashed the gun barrel back into Jamey's ear, "BLAMMO!!!"

The three women screamed and jerked forward out of instinct before stopping themselves—all in tandem. Jamey was now sobbing uncontrollably, eyes closed. In turn, Ray narrowed his eyes, now in full predation mode. "And! You certainly wouldn't want that! Now would you?" This last question was a growl. The women took an instinctive step backward.

Ray reverted to his cajoling voice again. "OK, then, here's the deal. We all are going to the computer in the family room, single-file." He pivoted toward the desk where the laptop was plugged in and the women slowly moved that way, hands in the air. He followed, with Jamey in tow. Once in the room he jerked Jamey to his side, practically strangling the boy in his elbow grip so he could safely point the gun at the bigger threat, the three women before him.

"Good, now Julianne, sit your monkey ass down there. Good. You other two bitches, stand against the wall. That's it. Now, Julianne, you're going to do a money transfer on your bank account. And quickly." He wagged the gun into Jamey's throat and watched triumphantly as Julianne pulled up her account and typed in her password.

CHAPTER 49

As soon as the call cut out on Officer Morris, he redialed the number, but it went immediately to voicemail. He tried again but got the same results. He asked the neighbor if he knew where Doug was headed but the man didn't know. By then another squad car had arrived with two other officers, so as they went up the stairs to the apartment, Officer Morris explained everything he knew about the situation. Once in the apartment he started a search of drawers and memo pads and phone lists of any kind, while the other officers gathered witness statements. Eureka -- Officer Morris found an address book that listed a sister named Julianne who lived in Portland. He also found Doug's listing. He engaged dispatch to check out both addresses immediately. Dispatch subsequently contacted the Portland police, who agreed to send out a patrol car to investigate.

*****

Doug parked a block away from Julianne's house, knowing that if Ray saw him coming it would trigger a series of events he didn't want to imagine. As he and Salli made their way swiftly and silently to the house, he saw an unfamiliar car parked just beyond the driveway and surmised it likely was Ray's. Of course the lowlife would have switched cars to make a getaway. Doug paused, gesturing for Salli to stay quiet with a finger over his mouth in a Shhh motion as his eyes scanned the area. She stopped and stayed at his side, step by step and on full alert as he slunk forward in a slight hunch. He first tried to peer through the front room window, but the blinds were down so he motioned her to creep behind him to try the next lighted window. But as they crept past the windowless front door, Salli stopped, staring into the wood with her ears straight up and the hair on her back and neck at a bristle. Doug knew instantly that meant Ray stood inside, and that something bad was about to happen.

He knew he shouldn't just burst through the door since he had no idea where everyone was and what peril they were in. So he gave Salli a "trust me, follow me" look and continued walking around the house to the kitchen window. He hunched down and carefully looked in and saw what he'd hoped beyond hope he wouldn't see. Over in the family room there was Ray holding a gun to Jamey's head. Alisha and Mary stood with palms raised in front of him, while Julianne sat at the computer looking terrified yet determined.

Thankfully, Doug had often helped with yard work and landscaping at Julianne's house, so he quickly could think of a couple advantages he could leverage. He knew his way around in the dark, and he had a key to their back door. He crept around to it, carefully unlocked it without making a sound, and—with another Shhh sign (unneeded, it seemed, based on the serious look Salli threw back his way)—they padded silently down the hallway to the master bedroom. Doug knew another door from the master led to the family room, where the danger was unfolding. Listening at that closed door, he heard Ray giving instructions to Julianne. From his vantage through the kitchen window, he knew Ray was facing away from the door he lurked behind, so—giving Salli a cautious look—he carefully turned the handle and inched the door ajar enough to see. Salli stayed motionless but alert at his side.

The way Ray was manhandling him, Jamey was the only one who saw the door subtly slip open. Doug met his astonished and relieved gaze with an urgent finger to his lips that made it clear to the boy he needed to pretend he hadn't seen anything. Salli's tail raised higher and her ears bent forward to likewise signal "don't make a move, we're on it" to the terrified child.

Seeing Jamey in such peril sent Doug's heart beating so fast, it deafened him. He stepped back into the bedroom to pull together his thoughts and resolve. He knew the boy couldn't fake not knowing for long. Salli backed up with him into the shadows, but instead of looking to her master for instruction, she kept her eyes fixed completely and calmly on Ray, tracking his every move.

Then Ray broke the relative silence of quiet sniffles and sobs emanating from the boy. "There ya go! That's real good, Julianne. You did great for an ignorant fool, I'm actually very proud of you, you did the simplest fucking thing! Now all I have to do is go to my investment account and pull out the money you just put there. See, since I'm a signer... mwhaa!" He chortled and wrenched up Jamey's neck to kiss the traumatized child on the head, keeping the gun steadily pointed at the temple of the completely unnerved child. "Ain't that great, boy!"

He then transmogrified the smile to a sneer and turned towards Alisha and Mary, still standing by the wall, hands still raised as if to protect the boy with their submissiveness.

At this, Salli padded silently toward the open door, her hair standing straight up and her mouth dropping open slightly—waiting for what she knew was coming.

CHAPTER 50

The Portland police cruiser idled down the street toward Julianne's house. The two officers weren't expecting much; their shift had been thankfully uneventful, and this last call didn't sound much different from all the others that had come to naught. As they neared the address, they saw a car parked just past the driveway on the street, outside the glow of any streetlight. The officer in the passenger seat pointed it out as slightly unusual for an area where residents had plenty of garage and driveway space for their families and their many cars.

Still, this registered as a mere blip on the officers' suspicion radar. As they reached the front door, the senior officer reached out to ring the doorbell, but his partner stopped him with a hand across the chest. She pointed silently to the key sticking out of the lock.

They put their hands on their weapons and listened at the door for a few seconds. When a gunshot and scream burst out from behind the door, they both drew their guns and rushed in.

The senior officer immediately planted, shouting "Don't move!" as he aimed his gun at the blur of action before him. His partner flanked to his right.

CHAPTER 51

Having turned his gaze on Mary and Alisa, Ray curled his face into its most evil smirk and jauntily jerked his head back and forth between them for a moment, whispering "Eenie, meenie miny moe..." He stopped and stared into Alisha's eyes with his most heinous expression. "Aha," he said breathlessly, "you must be the 'tiger's toe.'!" His volume rose. "Oh Alisha my dear...you know how it is. I just can't help myself—This one's for Doug and your stupid. fucking. dog."

He slowly turned the gun from the boy's head and aimed at Alisha. Then squeezed the trigger.

But Salli was a step ahead of him. Having watched for the opening she knew was coming when he started playing with Alisha; in an instant she had powerfully exploded from the bedroom door. In one swift motion she bit down with all her force on Ray's right hand. As the sound of the crushing bones pierced the stunned silence of the room, the gun fired.

Ray screamed and writhed in uncomprehending horror and pain as Salli mangled his wrist and hand.

The bullet that fired went wide right of its intended target: Alisha. As Ray fell, Jamey was able to squirm out of his loosening grasp and run to Mary and Alisha. Ray flailed about screaming, tumbling over Julianne onto the desk, where Julianne still sat. Julianne leapt backward, tossing the chair askew as she dashed to join Jamey and the others huddling low by the wall.

Salli, still holding on to what was left of Ray's hand, rolled over the desk and onto the floor, pulling Ray with her. The gun had also hit the desk when it fell from his hand and now lay on the floor next to the desk. Salli began to violently shake Ray's mutilated arm, causing Ray to scream in greater agony. Meanwhile Doug had burst into the room just in time to see two police officers run through the front door. He stopped short, as the male officer planted himself in the center of the living room, aiming his gun toward the ruckus on the floor.

Doug yelled and pointed toward Ray: "That's the guy trying to kill us!"

The officer spun toward Doug now, yelling, "Police! Get your hands up and hold still, everyone!"

Salli released her jaws from Ray's destroyed arm. The officer was now distracted by the aggressive canine standing over the mangled man, mouth open and making a low growling sound. The injured man was gawping at his bloody arm and hand, puzzling over the hand that hung dangling, barely still attached by skin and a few tendons.

But in a flash Ray snatched at the gun with his left hand and fired, hitting the cop in the chest. The officer had his vest on, but the impact of the bullet spun him around, leaving him vulnerable for the second shot Ray fired to hit him in the small of his back. The bullet tore through his lower body and came to rest in his lungs. The action was a blur, but Salli made sure there wasn't a third shot.

The second officer advanced from the periphery, gun drawn, shouting at Ray to drop the weapon, as Ray started to stand and turn the weapon toward the female cop. But as Ray struggled to rise without a free hand to push his maimed body up with, Salli lunged again. With a forceful bite and shake, she tore off the skin, muscle and cheek of Ray's face. The sound was wet and awful. He shrieked in rage and torment, flinging his left arm to hit the dog with the force of momentum and the heft of the metal weapon in his fist. The sweeping blow of pure rage managed to throw Salli a few feet from him, and he instantly fired a shot at her as she tumbled into the corner.

The hasty shot had flown far from the mark but

Ray was on his feet by now and taking new aim. The side of his face slapped like a wet rag against his neck as he spun toward Doug, his exposed jaw and gums grimacing like something out of a graphic horror movie. Doug lurched forward in blind hope of diverting the next shot, but once again Salli had reacted more quickly. She'd come out of her roll to the wall and flipped back like a spring toward Ray Allen, landing on him jaws first, tearing a chunk out of his thigh like it was cotton candy.

As he howled in new pain, he dropped to his knees and tried to focus the gun again at the beast but his sight was blurred now and as soon as the dog was clear of the perpetrator, the second officer fired two bulls-eye shots into Ray Allan's chest, hurling him backward to collapse over himself in a twisted heap. Salli quickly leapt back forward and grabbed the gun out of his hand and dropped it safely on the other side of the room, then sat at attention by it, panting happily.

The officer who'd shot Ray then shouted to everyone else in the room: "Nobody move, get your hands up!" Everyone complied except Jamey, who ran and hid behind the sofa, crying and shaking in the fetal position. Salli trotted over to him and gave him a few licks on the hands and the head, which drew him out of his fetal curl so he could cradle the dog's head in his lap, his arms wrapped around her in a tight embrace.

The officer called in to dispatch, her eyes on her fallen comrade and her weapon pointed toward everyone else. "Officer down! Shots have been fired, one suspect down. Four adults and one child in custody, requesting immediate back-up.

As soon as she finished, Doug spoke: "Officer, my name is Doug Thomas, and this is my wife Alisha. This is Julianne, my sister and this is Mary, my wife's sister. If I'm correct you were sent to check on Julianne Westphal's house and that is her right there." He pointed to Julianne. "Also, the piece of shit you shot is Ray Allan and I would bet you had that name on your initial call also. My other sister, who was sadly involved with this lowlife, though, is still missing!"

The officer relaxed a bit and said, "I'm sure you're correct sir but I have to be sure." A moment later two more police cars arrived followed closely by an ambulance. Once they'd triaged the injured officer and cleared everyone else, the focus turned to their panic about Melissa. Doug started peppering the officers with questions while the women tried to comfort and get information out of Jamey, but he was clearly in severe shock so they reverted to consoling him and getting him medical attention as well. In the midst of all this Salli jumped up from Jamey's lap and took off toward the front door.

Doug knew enough to follow her, and bring one of the additional officers with them. They hurriedly ran after her as she bolted directly to Ray Allan's car and started barking furiously at the trunk. The officer called back to a colleague in the house to get the keys as quickly as possible. They opened the trunk and to Doug's elation there was Melissa, alive and mostly unscathed. Her first words when the tape was pulled from her mouth were frantic: "Where's Jamey?"

Doug pulled her into a hug as the officer un-did the remaining tape. "It's okay, I promise. He's inside and he'll be OK. Salli has been…" He looked down and Salli was not there. He looked over at the officer, a new wave of anxiety waiting to grow in his chest: "Where'd my dog go?"

The officer replied: "Oh, didn't you notice? The dog darted back to the house at full speed. As soon as it saw that this lady was OK."

Doug hugged his sister for a second, then they hustled into the house. Melissa's eyes scoured the room to find Jamey, sitting next to Salli with his arms wrapped tightly around the dog. Melissa ran over to comfort her son, holding him close and trying to be strong for him as he sat crying in her arms. Salli sat right next to the pair, still vigilantly on watch.

Doug grasped onto his sister Julianne, who was

standing by him as they watched the tender reunion with shock and gratitude. Then he hurried over to Alisha, who was embracing her sister Mary. He rubbed Mary's shoulder as he wrapped his wife in a tight hug. He murmured into her ear, "I have never been as scared as I was when he pointed that gun at you."

"It was scary, I admit. I couldn't believe it when the bastard said, 'This is for Doug and that dog of yours.' He wanted you and Salli to live knowing he had killed your wife." She looked down at the crumbled body of Ray Allan just as he turned his head again exposing the grotesquely disfigured face. Alisha jumped back for a second, but then realizing he was completely finished, leaned over and grinned at him. "Fooled you, didn't we fucker!" She watched as the last flicker of life drained from his eyes.

Doug smiled at Alisha's extreme satisfaction. "He didn't know that Salli somehow sniffed out all he was up to. Can't say I understand it, but somehow, it happened, she knew exactly when she had an opening." He looked over and smiled at Salli, who immediately turned her head slightly to the side before hopping up and trotting over to Doug and Alisha, who dropped down joyfully to their knees and hugged her close.

CHAPTER 52

As things wrapped up in the house and the medics had patched everyone up, Doug then realized that the first officer into the house had died from his injuries at the scene. He went to the other officer and thanked her and gave his sincere condolences and promised to be at her partner's funeral. Soon after, he fulfilled that promise, accompanied by his wife and kids, his entire family and of course Salli.

Doug later also phoned and talked with Officer Morris from the Salem Police and thanked him for his persistence in finding out the additional information that had led to the Portland Police getting involved, a move that proved invaluable.

In the midst of so much chaos, it was decided that everyone should stay together for a while. Melissa, Jamey and Julianne stayed with Doug and Alisha. Robbie and Chloe came home also. So it was a very full house, but filled with kindness and caring that helped heal the many wounds caused by Ray Allan. Jamey especially benefited from having Robbie and Chloe nearby; kids have a way to cut through the crap and get to the heart, which accelerates healing, Melissa thought.

Mary stayed with her brother Allen and Jennifer and the two girls. She was bombarded with questions from Allen and especially the two girls, but it helped her cope with the ordeal.

After a few days both groups got together and decided on a date and time for Clark's funeral. The remembrance was set for the following Saturday, with a reception following at the Oregon Bank conference center. The family focused all their energies to arrange a celebration that would be long remembered, and with the help of all the employees from the Oregon Bank it had all the earmarks of accomplishing that.

The media got wind of Salli's involvement and immediately descended upon Doug and Alisha, wanting interviews and statements and any video footage. But they got nada: This time the details of the news story were kept private, fittingly since it was a very personal matter and the family had decided to stay quiet about it.

Doug did make a statement to the press; it simply said, "Please respect our privacy at this time and understand that our family and Salli need to heal from this devastating ordeal." For a few months after that announcement, the media, reporters and paparazzi tried everything to get some tidbit of a story. They ambushed and cajoled the kids to talk or take unwanted photos, even, but thankfully nothing really ever came of it, except for a few 'ragmag' articles. One that particularly amused the family was that Salli was an alien from another planet put here in a superman capacity to save the world. Many laughs and jokes (including the occasional cape) would come from that one.

CHAPTER 53

The day of the funeral arrived, and it all transpired as the family expected. Clark's service, held at the church that he and Julianne attended, was jammed with family, friends, fellow employees and clientele. Many people spoke of Clark and his kindness, his business savvy, fairness, friendliness and caring nature. But it was Doug's tribute to the man who lived by his sister's side with boundless unconditional love and support that left most everyone in tears.

The service ended with Julianne and family thanking everyone who came, by way of a receiving line. After Julianne felt she'd thanked everyone properly, she and Doug joined the rest of the family at the celebration of life. Everyone was eating and drinking and reminiscing about Clark. His widow seemed pleased with the festivities, and Doug even remarked to Alisha that he thought it was very cathartic for her. Then Doug got a surprise phone call, showing the screen to Alisha after his first shock of recognition: It was the Salem Police. "Whoah. I guess they probably have news about Ray Allan; I'll take this out in the hall." He moved out the door and answered his phone. It was once again Officer Ryan Morris. Doug had asked him to keep him informed of the investigation, and true to his word, he was doing just that.

Authorities had been able to conclusively identify Ray Allan as James Alton of Bakersville, CA. As a youth he had many scrapes with the law and a number of misdemeanors on his record. James Alton had just one felony: a case of animal cruelty, a charge classified as a felony based on the grotesque nature of the cruelty. He was 18 at the time.

A few years after that charge, though, James Alton simply disappeared. But now, with the help of dental records and DNA, they knew that Ray Allan was in fact James Alton. The police had also picked up his partner "Jackson" by tracing back the phone number that Ray had called many times. The partner's actual name was Larry Jackson. With his cooperation, it was determined that Alton had been involved in at least three other similar con games, one involving a woman who went missing and had yet to be found. In another, a family member had been murdered and Alton had managed to abscond scot-free with the life insurance money. Officer Morris shared further information with Doug about Alton's M.O., leaving Doug shaking his head at the fact that some people in this world are capable of such evil; and one such piece of information was of particular interest to him, as it made him reflect on Mary.

Something you should know, Mr. Thomas," the officer said, "is that this type of grifter, the one who's also a psychopathic criminal, is generally an expert at making sure his stories are foolproof, but inevitably there ends up being at least one simple slip-up that brings them down. And in this case, I think that's the fact that he used the exact same phrase to two members of your family; as soon as they connected those dots, it ultimately led to the perp's demise. Okay, I think that's all the information I have at this time, but if I can be of any more help, please call."

"Thank you, Officer Morris, you've been a great help." He hung up, returned to the celebration and found Alisha.

"Was it who you expected?"

"Yea, it was the Salem Police."

"Learn anything?"

"Quite a bit, but let's talk later. This isn't the place to discuss the findings about that scumbag."

She smiled and said, "You're right, but the mystery is oh so enticing." She leaned in and kissed him.

Doug then made his way around the room socializing, talking with a few people before he spotted Mary. She was standing on an outside deck, by herself, overlooking the Portland city view. It was a cold day but at the moment there was no rain. Doug quickly went to his table and took Alisha's wrap from the chair and went outside to offer it to Mary. She turned and smiled as he approached with the offering.

"Hi there sis-in-law! It's a little cold out here so I thought you could use this while Alisha is inside all warm and cozy." He draped the wrap over her shoulders and she pulled it tight.

"It's been a great service and celebration. I think it's been good for Julianne," she offered, as her eyes slowly scanned the cityscape.

"Yes, I agree. Hey, I thought you might be interested to know I got some info back about Ray Allan. Seems his real name was James Alton; a psychopath loser that had done this many times before. They think one of the other times resulted in the disappearance of the poor woman he was conning at the time; she's been missing for years. They think he murdered her but can't find the body. Oh and in one of his other scams, a family member was killed and he got away with the life insurance money. Sound a little close to our situation?"

Mary paused for just a moment before responding: "Lord! Do you think he had something to do with Clark's death?"

"I have to admit now that it's probable. But! I don't think the family needs to know that, especially since we don't know for sure. Melissa is going through enough guilt without piling that on top of it all, and the others just don't need to know." She nodded numbly before he continued. "You know, Mary, the police were very impressed by you, in that you saw the flaw in Ray's game. So am I for what it's worth. You're kind of the hero!"

Mary looked at Doug, her eyes filling with tears. "Doug, I have something that I need to tell you that happened..."

But Doug broke her off: "You know, that sonofabitch actually had drugged some members of the other families so he could take advantage of them?! He'd slip them a drug called Ketamine, a date rape drug that pretty much renders a person helpless. After he took advantage of them, he'd hold the shame over their head to bilk more money out of them. Can you believe it?"

He spanned his thoughtful gaze across the expanse of the city and slowly shook his head before he went on. "If that had been the case with our family... " He didn't turn to notice Mary's utter silence, and continued. " I'd almost hope it just remained untold. It certainly wouldn't be anyone's fault and it definitely wouldn't do anybody any good to know about it. In fact, that bastard roasting in hell would probably even enjoy it!" Doug shook his head, disgusted, contemplating for a few seconds before he jerked around to face Mary and said, "Well, enough of that joyful conversation! Let's go in and have a drink, a drink to Clark!"

A stream of tears spilled from Mary's knowing eyes, She smiled at Doug and hugged him, saying, "Yes. Let's. Sounds good."

Doug wrapped an arm around her and they went back to the celebration of life.

*****

Over the next few months, Melissa and Jamey both benefitted from therapy sessions. During this time, Julianne also participated in group therapy through a lost spouses group, which proved to be a life-saver for her. Julianne sold the house in Portland and moved into a condo near where Mary lived. Allen and Jennifer continued their normal life of raising the kids and being the contented all-American family. Doug and Alisha got back to a normal life with the kids and Salli.

Blissfully, the media buzz gradually died down, and life became normal again. The Ray Allan incident was fully behind them, and with each day it seemed to fade further into the mists of bad memory. They started to feel like a family again, a feeling that was relished by them all.

CHAPTER 54

Flash forward two years. They had gone by pretty uneventfully for the family. Salli put her super-hero status behind her and enjoyed just being the happy family pet. That didn't mean, however, that on a few occasions she didn't help the family make some important decisions, though.

One evening, shortly after Robbie had gotten his driver's license, he was heading out to cruise around with some friends. But Salli made it very clear that she did not want him to go, blocking the door and barking at him when he tried to step around her. Based on that, Doug made the split decision that Robbie would stay home that night, much to the chagrin of the new driver, who thought how stupid it was for the family *dog* to determine if he could go out or not! Nothing happened that night to make anyone think it was a miracle for Sallie to have stopped him, but Doug knew in his heart that she *sensed* something bad and that he had made the correct decision. Sure enough, years later Robbie admitted that the night she stopped him, he had been headed to a party involving activities that a sixteen-year-old would be better to avoid.

Overall, life had returned to normal for everyone.

Julianne was living alone in her condo and volunteering on various committees. She was a very active participant in the lost spouse therapy group. The service and support had become a priority in her life, and she dedicated a great deal of her life and money to the cause. Clark's will had made sure that she would never have to work, and she was eternally grateful for the chance to contribute her time to a meaningful cause. She held Clark in her heart till the day she died. She would later marry again, but held an eternally special place in her heart for Clark.

Mary had continued her career as a flight attendant and traveled all across the globe. She kindled a romance with a male flight attendant after about a year of the family trauma and they'd moved in together and travelled together as much as they could. Mary enjoyed her new lease on life and had come to terms with the ordeal Ray Allan had put her through. She never revealed her "Ray secret" and felt comfortable with that decision for the rest of her life.

Melissa eventually went back to work at Ricoh's Women's Wear and became the manager of the Salem store. She had great success as a manager, and after a few years became a regional manager in charge of training. She moved from the apartment she had shared with Ray and was able to purchase a home of her own. It was a few years before she felt she could trust a man again, but eventually she did start back dating, but never without doing extensive background checks on her prospects.

Jamey, who'd gone through so much so young, continued to have bad dreams for years, but thanks to steady therapy, a supportive family, and growing maturity, grew to deal with the trauma much better. Eventually, it became a distant memory that he could healthily live with. He went on to become a star athlete in high school and college, and eventually started a family of his own.

Doug and Alisha never relinquished their shared promise not to allow life to get in the way of their passion for each other. They lived and loved happily ever after, even renewing their vows on their 25th wedding anniversary, and promising they would renew them again on their 50th...which they did.

CHAPTER 55

But a few months after Salli's 6th birthday, Doug noticed something a bit concerning. She would tilt her head quickly to the right, in rapid succession three or four times. Once he saw her actually whining while doing it, as if it hurt. He immediately plopped down onto the floor with her and started rubbing behind her ears, and again she tilted her head once more as if it pained her. As he pet her lovingly, his fingers fell upon a spot behind her ear that he hadn't noticed before. It was hard like a growth, long and slender and progressing down and into her neck. He told Alisha about it and said he wanted to take her into the vet to have it looked at. They both agreed and decided to have an overall check-up of their beloved furry friend while they were at it.

The next morning Alisha called the veterinarian office and made an appointment for the coming Friday morning. She explained about the hardness behind her ear and also told them they wanted the wellness check-up.

When Friday came, Doug was understandably

anxious. Any kind of unknown condition is scary, but when you feel a growth, it automatically brings cancer into your thought process. When they arrived, both went into the exam office and when the vet started examining the growth behind Salli's ears, they couldn't help but notice that the vet got a rather puzzled look on her face.

When Doug asked what she was thinking she replied, "I don't really know. This has the feel of a growth, but it actually feels like it's growing within, kind of like a root from a tree. It actually feels like this is growing from somewhere inside her neck or head and is traveling around looking for something. I think we better take an x-ray of the area and see what it shows."

"Can we do that now?"

"Yes. We have an x-ray facility in the back. We'll take Salli back there and get a couple of neck and head shots and see what we can find. It shouldn't take more than a half hour or so and you guys can wait in the lobby till we're finished and then we'll come and get you."

After about 40 minutes the vet came out to usher them back again, where Salli wagged her tail in happiness to see them. They stood on either side of her on the examination table, which had always ironically been one of Salli's favorite places (contrary to most dogs). They'd always figured it was because the height made it one of the few times she could look them straight in the eye.

The vet proceeded to update them. "OK, here is the x-ray and I will be honest, I don't quite know what to make of it. If you look here, this is what we are feeling, but it seems to intertwine into her neck and head. And if you look at this," she pointed to the brain and touched on three different areas, "you see the same kind of mass growing behind her ear in all these other places in the brain. It's odd but it's almost as if this growth is moving into her brain."

She looked at the rightfully worried Doug and Alisha and continued calmly. "There's no reason to panic right now, as nothing looks immediately ominous. I recommend we put in a referral to the OSU veterinary clinic in Corvallis. They have specialists there that will be much more familiar with this than I am. They also have an imaging department that can do way more than we can here." Doug and Alisha began to relax, just a little as the vet concluded her counsel: "I suspect they'll do an MRI and be able to tell you a lot more from that. I'll call in the referral today so you can then call them to make an appointment. It's also good to know that this type of case may be looked at as an experimental procedure, which will give you a huge break because they absorb much of the cost for teaching and experimentation purposes. Rest assured, I will plant that seed with them."

After that confusing update, Doug and Alisha took Salli home with some pain pills and a hearty dose of resolve. Later in the day they called the Oregon State University Veterinary Clinic, located on the college campus in Corvallis. An appointment was made for the following Wednesday. Now they had to simply wait. But in the meantime, Doug made a call to Dr. Alex Smythe on the idea that he might be even more familiar with whatever this might be and could share some advice and guidance.

The doctor was avuncular when he heard he was calling. "Well, hello Doug! It is nice to hear from you. How's the family doing?

"Hi Alex! The family is doing well. Everybody seems to be going in the right direction and everyone is happy. Except for me right now."

"What's up? Not like you to be the one not doing well."

"Well, technically it's not me, but Salli. We just took her to the vet after finding a lump behind her ear. The vet x-rayed it, and what she found was a bit ... well, disturbing."

"Disturbing? How?"

The doctor listened for the next twenty minutes

as Doug told the full story as best he could. Dr. Smythe asked a few questions along the way, and they ended the call with Doug giving Dr. Smythe the phone number of the vet they'd gone to, so he could get a copy of the x-ray. He promised Doug that he'd call him on Monday after he reviewed everything.

The next day was difficult for Doug and Alisha, who simply couldn't banish all the worry from their minds. Finally, on Monday afternoon Dr. Smythe called and talked with Doug.

"Thank you SO much for reaching out. What did you find, Alex?"

Dr. Smythe's tone was a bit too quizzical for Doug's comfort. "Well, this is really a strange one. I even brought in a colleague of mine that knows far more about these types of things than even I do. What we've concluded is that this... growth, if that's what it is, appears to have no origin. It's as though there are tentacle-like structures– for lack of a better term–growing through the brain, but we can't identify a starting point. I'm afraid that brave dog of yours will need to have much more extensive imaging done to determine exactly what is going on. So, what I would like to propose, with your permission of course, is that I contact Oregon State Veterinary and ask to be involved in this diagnosis. That way, I think I would be able to ascertain a better conclusion for you. Will that be OK with you Doug? I, of course have this all approved with your original vet. She is on-board 100%, as long as we share our findings with her."

"Of course. And I can't thank you enough; this is really above and beyond what you should be doing."

"Nonsense! I know firsthand that Salli is special, and so are you two! And from a strictly physiological point of view, I'm intrigued because the necessary testing could explain some of her abilities. All the same, it's important not to get ahead of ourselves, okay? Let's find out what all is going on first, and then we can talk more intelligently about what should be done about it."

After Doug hung up he went immediately to Alisha to update her. They embraced each other in a comforting hug, bracing themselves for whatever may come.

CHAPTER 56

The morning of the Wednesday appointment found Doug and Alisha somber and worried. Nevertheless, they steadied themselves, put on their bravest faces (for Salli as much as themselves), and headed into the office, where they were comforted by the marvelous treatment they got from the entire staff.

The receptionist made a point to come around the desk to greet Salli, and when the assistant came out to take Salli back for the imaging, she greeted all three of them with hugs. When Doug handed a credit card to the receptionist with the explanation "so that we don't forget after this is over," she shook her head and said, "Oh, that won't be necessary. Dr. Smythe and the University are handling all the costs. Don't worry, the vet will tell you more when you go in." Alisha had overheard all this from her seat in the waiting area; Doug smiled over her way with a subtle surprised and grateful shake of his head.

Time creeped by as they waited over an hour separated from their beloved dog undergoing the scan. Finally the vet came out to tell them the imaging was completed, and that Salli would be awake in a few minutes. They could go back to be with her as soon as she woke up.

Alisha asked, "What'd you find out?"

The vet looked at them both squarely and said, "It's too early to tell you what a diagnosis would be. But I will tell you that the tumor has spread throughout the brain. But we don't know what it is, or why it is, or what it is doing to her. We are conferring right now with Dr. Smythe and one of his colleagues." Just then an assistant came out and told the doctor that Salli was awake. "Perfect! Why don't you two go back with her for now and my team will get back with right after we assess the results more conclusively."

They hurried back to the room where Salli was just waking up from the anesthetic. As soon as she saw them she began wagging her tail, even though she was still clearly still a little woozy. They cooed and surrounded her on both sides, kissing and petting her while trying to veil their anxiety about what answers might be coming their way from the veterinary team. They tried to hold their deepest fears at bay and dosed out plenty of love on Salli while they waited.

After 40 minutes, Doug's phone rang and he saw that it was Dr. Smythe calling. He looked at Alisha, tightened his jaw and answered, "Hi Alex,

I assume you are calling to give us some news about Salli." Alisha wrapped a hand through the crook of his elbow and nuzzled up close, one hand still stroking Salli's heart-shaped Pitbull head.

Doug was listening and she couldn't quite hear Dr. Smythe. Doug said, "Yes, I am. Also Alex, Alisha is here, so I'm going to put you on speaker so she can hear too." He switched to speaker and Alisha nestled her head deeper into his neck to steady him as they both listened. "OK Alex," Doug said, further steadied by his wife's presence. "You're on speaker. Shoot."

"Hi Alisha, I'm sorry you have to go through this."

Alisha had tears in her eyes already but replied, "Thank you Alex. Thank you for a lot of things..."

"Of course, my pleasure. Now, OK...I know there is only one question you need and want answered. So I'm going there first. Salli has a tumor that has spread and intertwined throughout her entire brain. And, there is really nothing we can do. Surgery would be futile and risky enough that she probably wouldn't even survive it. The best thing you guys can do is take her home and give her all the love you do every day. I'm sure you will both know when the time will be right."

Doug took a sharp breath in, putting a hand up to stroke Alisha's hair as her tears grew into a convulsive spontaneous sob from the shock. He drew up the strength from her to continue speaking into the phone speaker, though his voice came out sounding weak and beaten in his ears. "How long do you think she has?"

Dr. Smythe hesitated only briefly, but it felt like an eternity to the stricken couple. "A matter of days or weeks, I'm afraid." Alisha emitted an audible sob and Salli lifted her head from beneath her stroking hand, as if to console the hand that had been consoling her. Time moved slowly; the ticking of the clock in the room boomed in Doug's ears.

Alex continued: "The tumor has taken up so much room in her head that the pressure she feels must be almost unbearable. You of course will be given some medicine to administer for her pain. Doug, Alisha, I'm so very sorry to share this news. She's the most special of all the dogs I've met in my life—I mean that and I know you know I mean it. And I know you and your family have loved her to the absolute maximum, and that she's returned that love in spades, if not more so."

"Thanks Alex, thanks for being the one to break this terrible news to us. It means a lot." He took an unstable breath in to steady himself again.

"Of course, I've been more than happy to. Listen, go home and just be together and comfort her. Then call me back in a couple of days. There's a bit more we need to talk about, but right now the biggest priority is for you and your family to come to terms with what's coming."

They ended the call and Doug slipped his phone back into his pocket. The three of them sunk into a tender group hug, with Salli giving them both consoling looks from her eye-level position on the exam table. After a few minutes they daubed their eyes, gathered up their dear dog from the table, retrieved her pain medicine and went home.

*****

As promised, a few days later Doug called Dr. Smythe back. "Hi Alex. I'm calling you back as we discussed. It's been an emotional few days, but we're accepting reality as best we can."

"How's she doing?"

"The pills make her lethargic, but she still is the same sweet dog."

"That's good. And I'm glad to hear you sounding as stalwart as you can be. It seems like that means the time is right to talk to you a bit more about Salli's tumor. All of us on the care team, I have to say, have never come across anything like it before. And as I'm sure you know, between us there's a good amount of combined experience and knowledge. The truth is, for a tumor to grow and implant itself like what we see in Salli is an absolute phenomenon."

Doug sat silent and Dr. Smythe continued. "The care team has discussed at length Salli's 'abilities,' which I myself observed, and that the news reports suggested, and we've debated whether this tumor could be related to that. I have to tell you, all of us *do* believe they're somehow connected. Now to be clear, we don't know *what* that connection is precisely, but from the scans we have reason to believe that the growth started in her brain at a very young age and somehow changed the patterns of her brain. That very well may have given her abilities that a normal functioning canine brain wouldn't have. But it's inconclusive how the continued growth of the brain mass may have changed those 'abilities' over time."

Doug was happy to feel a slight smile grace his face for some reason. He replied, "I see. So ... what are you asking, Alex?"

"Just this: When her time comes, OSU would like to be allowed to perform an autopsy, for you to allow us to remove her brain and the entire tumor, and use it for study and research." He paused and continued in a more impassioned tone. "Between us, Doug, I believe whatever is in her could hold answers and new paths that could be pivotal for the future—not only in dogs, but related to human development also."

Doug's smile was now beaming. With no hesitation he said, "Absolutely, doctor! I think Salli would want that too; it would be her chance to continue helping people for a long time to come. Thank you, I just think this is the best possible outcome to a heartbreaking situation."

"Thank you, Doug. Of course her remains would be cremated and given to you for her burial. And everything I've discussed will be taken care of financially by the university."

"Thank you for that, Alex. I'll keep you informed as things unfold on this end ... not to be too vague about it, but you know what I mean."

"I do, Doug. My best to you and Alisha and Salli during this time."

Doug's smile far exceeded the end of the call. He went out to find Salli immediately: It was play and snuggle time indeed.

CHAPTER 57

Three weeks on, the sad moment arrived. Salli had been moving more slowly and her head was in the tilted position almost continually. One morning she didn't get up for their morning walk at all. Doug curled up on the floor next to her as she lay in her bed and began petting her. He could feel the emotions piling up inside of himself as he reached for her pain pills in his robe pocket.

He staved off tears while opening the bottle. Just then, Salli gently lifted her paw and laid across Doug's arm as she turned her eyes up to his. He'd seen that expressive, all-knowing and deeply penetrating look from her enough times to read it well. He knew instantly that she was telling him, it was time. He slowly stroked one ear, murmuring: "Is it time, baby girl?"

She gave a small tail wag, to one side and then back again, never shifting her eyes from Doug's. Her empathetic look of love was all the answer he needed. "OK, but you have to know, this isn't going to be easy and I would just about do anything else in the world." He leaned down and kissed her on the top of her head. He then called Alisha in a tone that brought her into the room already crying.

"It's time?" She breathed deeply to steady herself.

"Yea, she just told me. I'm going to tell Chloe and then call Robbie to come home."

"Should we call the others?"

"No...this should be just us."

*****

He first called Robbie, who was staying in an apartment with two other roommates while they attended the local community college. He said he would come home immediately. Doug then went to Chloe's room and sat with her. After a tearful moment followed by a calming talk, Chloe went down to join her mother. Doug then called the phone number that Alex Smythe had arranged for him to call. Dr. Ramsey was the vet that had been put in charge of the final arrangements and autopsy. Doug had met her and they had set up a number for him to call when it was time.

"Hello, Doug."

"Hi Dr. Ramsey."

"Is it time?"

"Yes."

"OK, I'll be there in about forty five minutes... I'm sorry Doug." She disconnected the call.

Doug went to be with his girls. He reflected on how much he'd always loved saying or thinking that about the triad of his wife, daughter and dear doggie. "His girls." Now there would be one less of them. When he entered the room both Lish and Chloe were crying, as they petted and talked lovingly to Salli.

Doug put on a happy face for them and said, "Hey, let's not make this sad. Salli doesn't want that. Let's remember the good times, hey?" "His girls" perked up at the idea of making Salli's end a celebratory affair, and he joined them at their vigil as they all started telling stories of happy times—all the while surrounding their sweet and special canine friend with snuggles and kisses and tender strokes behind her ears and under her chin.

Robbie arrived after about ten minutes, completing the pack. The full family of five spent another half hour recalling and relishing all the good times they'd had with Salli, focused firmly on laughs and smiles. Salli lay relaxed and happy, her tail still contentedly wagging slowing back and forth.

When the doorbell rang, quiet fell over everything. Doug gave Salli one more comforting chin scratch, then stood up, swallowed hard and said, "Please say your goodbyes now, everyone. I'd like to be with alone with her when she goes." Everyone looked at him with a look of complete understanding.

"I'll wait outside with the doc till you're ready."

He made his way to the door and joined Dr. Ramsey on the threshold outside, explaining that they needed to wait a bit til the rest of the family was done bidding Salli their farewells. After about ten minutes the door opened and Alisha emerged with a glassy-eyed child under each arm. She nodded bravely to Doug.

Doug gave his family a bear hug and then a stalwart nod as he released them and ushered Dr. Ramsey into the house. The vet greeted Salli with soothing tones as she approached her, patted her, prepared her materials and explained to Doug gently. I'll give her a sedative to calm her, then I'll step back outside while you say goodbye. Here's a newfangled pager, press this button when you're ready for me to return to administer the final medicine. Once I inject that, she'll succumb quickly."

She administered the shot of sedative and quietly retreated back out the front door. Doug gazed down tearfully at Salli and she returned his love with one last slight tail wag. He shifted from a sitting position to lay fully flat on the floor beside Salli's bed, curling his body around his canine friend and stroking her softly. He lay his head down on the floor and turned his face to meet her dimming eyes.

"Salli, you know you've been the best friend I could ask for. I love you as much as any human I've known and I'll miss literally everything about you…except maybe your snoring." He gave her a soft stroke under the chin and smiled broadly at her, which she managed to reciprocate with a tiny lick to his arm, even as the sedative did its work. *"A champion to the end,"* he thought and nuzzled her nose with his.

"I can't express how much I'll miss you! I *promise* … I promise I will never forget you. I'll never forget all you did for this family, and for so many others. You're my hero, you're a lot of people's hero. You are … what can I say? -- truly exceptional!"

He hugged her close for a while longer before pressing the button. Salli's breathing had slowed but she gave one tail twitch, which he took as a final demonstration of her love and devotion to him and his family.

Dr. Ramsey came in and, as Doug whispered

more loving kindnesses into Salli's ear, injected the euthanasia medication. Doug cried softly as his embracing arms felt Salli expel her last breath.

CHAPTER 58

They received Salli's ashes from Dr. Ramsey about four days after her final sleep. Everyone in the family agreed with the decision they made but wanted to be able to say goodbye. So on the first Sunday of March a celebration of life event was planned in the backyard of Doug and Alisha's home. In a shady back corner of the yard sat two chaise lounge chairs with a table in between. This was a favorite spot for Salli because when the family was outside she could lie under the table between the chairs and enjoy the company of whoever sat there. This spot was fittingly chosen to be the burial ground for her ashes.

Friends and family gathered at the house, including Dr. Alex Smythe, Dr. William Clark, Amy with her new husband and her daughter Maddie, and even Gino Vincini with his daughter Marisa and wife Maria. Sally the firefighter was there too, not to mention various friends and neighbors. Everyone had drinks in the house first, talking and getting acquainted for a while before Doug called everyone to the back yard.

As the group gathered in the back corner, where Doug had carved out a shallow grave in the shade, he asked if anyone wanted to say a word about Salli. For the next thirty minutes or more, a plethora of guests talked about the amazing dog and some of the interactions they'd had with her. When silence finally fell, Doug asked, "Anyone else?" Gino, who had been strangely quiet, raised his hand. Doug said, "Yes, Gino, would you like to say something?" And for the next ten minutes Gino gave a highly emotional tribute to a dog that he said *was now sitting in heaven with God's hand upon her head.* Doug then finished the tribute by spreading Salli's ashes in the shallow grave and covering them with the loose dirt.

Then, after Robbie and Chloe had filled a flute of champagne for everyone present, it was Doug's turn to speak: "Salli was called 'special' by a number of people, many of whom have just spoken. Certainly some of the experiences the rest of us had with her would confirm that statement. We don't know what made her so special, but I think it was in large part just the love of this family and the friends we're lucky enough to have. Today we celebrate the life of a dog that was loved by all of us, and who loved us un-conditionally. *That* is what made her special."

He raised his glass, his eyes shining. "So charge

your glasses and toast with me the amazing life of our dog Salli with an i!" They all sipped the champagne with glassy eyes and quietly dabbed tears...except for Gino, who cried openly and demonstratively. Doug strode over to put his arm around Gino and give him a grateful and supportive squeeze. The men exchanged a serious look and then a shared laugh before Doug turned back to the rest. "Alright, thank you all! Now let's go back inside and enjoy this time together--that's what Salli would want!" Everyone applauded and cheered Salli, then headed back into the house to tell more stories, enjoy all the amazing food that Alisha had prepared, plus all the bread, pastries and cannoli that Gino had contributed. As the convivial gathering continued, the sun set--casting its final shadow on the corner of the yard out back where someone had lain flowers on the newly honored gravesite.

CHAPTER 59

As the memorial celebration continued, the doorbell rang. Doug went to the door and opened it. In the threshold stood a young man in a police uniform. Doug asked quizzically, "Hi, may I help you?"

The young officer said, "Mr. Thomas?"

"Yes?"

"Sir, you don't know me, but I know you...or at least I know...or knew...your dog."

Doug looked at him rather dumbfounded, "Uhh, OK, I uhhh."

"Sir, I'm not making any sense and I apologize for that. About six years ago I broke into your house as an initiation into a gang. I was here to rob you of whatever I could get. And that's when I met your dog."

The happy din of the house turned to murmurs as rest of the family and friends gathered behind Doug in shared curiosity.

The officer continued humbly: "Sir, would you

mind if I intrude for a few minutes to tell my story?"

Doug was suddenly hit with a dose of understanding. He smiled and said, "Certainly, I'm sorry, come in and sit down." He gestured warmly to the couch and the group parted loosely to welcome the surprising new guest.

The officer nodded solemnly as he moved through the scattering throng. He took a seat on the sofa as everyone gathered around. He politely refused a glass of champagne and started his story.

"First, I'm Officer Samuel Johnston. And as I said, when I was approximately sixteen years old I was being initiated into a gang. The rite of passage, as I was told, was to break into a house and rob the inhabitants. I chose this house, but the truth is I was scared to death. The fact was, I didn't really want to join the gang but didn't feel like I had a lot of other choices. So, I came through the kitchen window over there, which was un-locked by the way." He winked at Doug. "I crouched and crept my way across the counter, quietly dropped down to the floor, and came face to face with your dog. How I didn't pee my pants right then still remains a mystery to me. I remember thinking at that instant that this was the stupidest thing I have ever done and that I wished I'd never even talked to those gang members."

Everyone chuckled and fell quiet again, enrapt by the tale.

"Her name was Sally, correct?"

Chloe answered from the corner: "Yea, Salli. With an i."

Office Johnston smiled at her and continued. "Alright then. Well Salli with an i never barked, growled, snarled or even changed her expression. She just stared, never taking her eyes off me. I froze, my eyes darting around as I pondered how to proceed. I had been given a doggie biscuit by one of my new found 'friends' and was told that if I was confronted by a dog to use this to befriend them. But she didn't budge, just continued that constant stare.

"Her unmoving gaze flummoxed me and for some reason I just asked the dog if she wanted me to leave. Her stare didn't shift, so after a moment I slowly put my arms behind me, holding her stare as I hoisted myself up onto the counter and backed away back toward the window, where I froze once more. As I'd retreated she'd risen up to place her front paws on the counter, but didn't pursue further –thankfully!—but just stood with that intent look fixed on me, her tail slowly wagging back and forth.

"I turned quickly and dropped back out of the

kitchen window and onto the ground. As I hightailed it off your property, I made your dog – and myself – a mental promise. And I kept it. As you can see, I found another life to pursue rather than a gang. I'm a cop now, but I spend as much time as I can working with kids, trying to keep them from making the wrong sort of choices that I almost did."

There were oohs and awwws and then a rousing round of applause. The young man blushed and answered a smattering of questions for a few minutes before he finally stood and looked back at Doug, saying quietly, "Well, because of the news coverage she so rightly deserved, I knew Salli was being buried today and I wanted to say to you face to face: I'm sorry for your loss. Sir, would you mind if I paid my respects to her?"

Doug stepped forward and put a hand on his shoulder. "Not at all, come with me." He led him to the back and pointed at the back corner. "Would you like to be alone?"

"Yes sir, if possible. She represents a sea of change in my life and I'd like to honor her privately, if you don't mind."

"Go ahead." Doug moved back to the house and gave him privacy.

Samuel walked slowly over to the fresh soil and knelt down beside it. "Hi, Salli. I would have liked to have known you properly. From what I have heard, and after the difference you made for me, it's clear you were really something else. I know I will never forget you. I came to say Thank You." He reached into his front shirt pocket and pulled out a lint-covered doggie treat, holding it up as if showing it to her. "I carry it, and you, with me on every shift." He reverently returned the talisman to his pocket, stood up and smiled down back at his salvation. "Sleep well."

After he returned inside, Doug walked him to the front door. He said his goodbyes to everyone in the room, then turned to Doug on the doorstep. "Thank you, Mr. Thomas."

"Call me Doug."

"Thank you Doug."

He waved and Doug returned the gesture saying, "Come back around sometime, won't you?"

"I'd like that." Officer Johnston smiled softly and walked away.

Doug watched as the young officer drove off, then returned to the celebration. As everyone continued their conversations and stories, Doug affectionately rubbed the bracelet around his left wrist, which led him to shoot a glance out the kitchen window to the back corner of the yard. The bracelet contained the ashes of Salli's heart, a touching gesture that Dr. Ramsey had made happen. Suddenly Alisha was next to him. He wiped the corner of an eye and wrapped an arm around her. The pair stood shoulder to shoulder as they gazed gratefully out at Salli's final resting place , a loving habit they would repeat countless times over the years to come.

The handmade headstone simply said,

"Exceptional".

Epilogue

The removal of the tumor and brain of Salli had proved a daunting task for the veterinary surgeons. The tumor had entwined her entire brain and even snaked down toward her heart and other internal organs. Never had the doctors seen such a complex and wide-reaching tumor. It was like an organ in itself, with a few larger, more prevalent tributaries of the tumor, with each of those forking off into as many as 20 smaller tributaries that stretched throughout her entire brain and body. The surgery took over 16 hours to remove the sum total of the sarcoma.

This amount of effort for a canine autopsy certainly wasn't standard, but it had been approved because of the scientific advances it might afford. Dr. Alex Smythe was on the team in charge of studying the tumor, along with the research specialists at Oregon State Veterinary Hospital. Through their research they determined that the origin, or core, of the tumor started deep in Salli's brain. Over time as the tumor had grown it appeared to have overtaken parts of her brain to control the functions of those areas. The researchers also concluded that the chemicals and enzymes that made up the tumor had greatly increased the biochemical reactions in her brain to a level that was completely unheard of in animals or even in humans.

To learn more, samples and findings were shared with a variety of research facilities across the country. Research was done at some of the highest levels across major medical facilities, and in each instance all the researchers involved grew excited by new findings. Dr. Smythe began working almost full-time on this research, and published a paper detailing how the level of the chemicals in the tumor could activate areas of the canine brain never before seen.

His paper caught the attention of many hospitals, clinics and veterinary drug companies—even a division of the U.S. weapons and wartime research. Interest to capitalize on the discovery grew around the world. For Dr. Smythe, it quickly became a full-time job in itself just to manage all the different proposals and requests from so many interested parties.

Then, one morning at the Oregon State Veterinary research center, an analyst working with Dr. Smythe found that a number of samples of the tumor were missing. More confounding and worrying still, hundreds of pages of findings, theories, conclusions and research had been stolen off the main computer. When Dr. Smythe heard the news, he went white: What did this breach mean, not just as a continuation of the remarkable story of Salli—but for the world.

Authors Note

Thank You for reading my story about a very special dog. Although there is research being done to learn more about the perception abilities of dogs, please remember that the story you just read is fiction. I am a huge fan of adopting dogs and feel strongly that adding a dog to your life can be a wonderful experience. But it's crucial to remain "eyes wide open" about dog adoption.

I've heard too many stories of people getting dogs because they think they'll arrive just as well-behaved as the dog in the movie or ad that led them to fall in love with the breed. When the TV series "Game of Thrones" was on the air, husky dogs skyrocketed in popularity, for example, with people thinking they would be magically blessed with the same regal and magnificent dog behavior portrayed in the series. But every dog is unique and requires loving training and attention and care. Pit Bulls are often adopted or purchased just for the look of being tough. There are a number of wrong reasons to adopt a dog.

Recently, I experienced a similar situation in my life. Two years ago we lost our 15-year-old family dog, Emma. She'd been a constant source and focus of love in our household, and two years after she succumbed, we decided to get another dog. In my mind I thought of it as "getting another Emma." This was totally unfair to the new arrival, and for a couple of weeks after bringing home Duffy, I really struggled to form a bond with him. My wife helped me see that I was the one being unfair and unreasonable. Duffy had every right to his own personality and abilities. After accepting that, I formed a unique relationship with my new companion, one totally different from what I'd shared with Emma, and he has firmly become part of the family—loved and appreciated in his own right. So keep in mind, every dog is special in its own way, and as an owner you have the responsibility to care for, protect and love them.

With dedicated training and proper care, a dog can become an integral part of a happy family life. Just remember the commitment you're making to the dog when you bring it home, and that every day you have to live up to that commitment.

"Money can buy you a fine dog, but only

love can make him wag his tail"
    Kinky Friedman